Praise

"*Auras* is a timeless and deeply moving collection of short fiction. In these poignant stories, Kevin Fitton illuminates the mysterious chambers of the human heart. Fitton renders his characters with such care and delicate craftsmanship that readers will be reminded of Andre Dubus and John Cheever. These are stories of grief and desire, of melancholy and atonement, and they leave no doubt that even in our darkest moments, our lives are still emanating a rare and hopeful light."
—Bret A. Johnston, internationally best-selling author of *Remember Me Like This*

"These stories, these joyful bursts of humanity, are the tonic we need, each story a thoughtful, utterly surprising voice in our ear conjuring new worlds; they snap into focus. Fitton writes with a jeweler's precision, yet unspools stories with effortless grace about love, understanding, compassion, confusion; his scope and heart are enormous. Here's how I felt: that I was sitting on a porch at perfect sunset and the stories had beckoned to step off into the night grass, into mystery, other lives. If you love Marilynne Robinson or Charles Baxter, *Auras* is your book."
— Doug Stanton, #1 New York Times Bestselling author of *Horse Soldiers, In Harm's Way, 12 Strong*

"The beautifully crafted stories of Kevin Fitton's *Auras* explore the fathomless intimate terrain of human relationships, seeking at every turn to uncover and understand the ways in which we try so desperately, and so often fail, to communicate—or even to know—what's in our own hearts. Fitton's characters are like family: beloved in all their flawed, broken, humbled, and endlessly striving humanity."

—Thisbe Nissen, author of *How Other People Make Love, Our Lady of the Prairie*, and *Osprey Island*

"Kevin Fitton's characters—pastors, parents, a math teacher who is also a mom and a thief, a steamboat ferryman—are always aspiring to do better, and much of the pleasure of reading his work is in rooting for their better angels and wondering when and where they'll succeed. Too wise a writer to believe in easy happy endings, Fitton is nonetheless attuned to the possibility of transformation. The pulse of human warmth running through these stories pulls the reader on from one to the next."

— Rachel Pastan, author of *In the Field*

"Readers, beware. The stories in Kevin Fitton's powerful new collection, Auras, contain strong, sometimes hurtful emotions. Faced with loss and disappointment, characters lash out, showing us the extremes that love will drive us to. And in the end, those characters are left with a greater, sometimes rueful, understanding of their own hearts—as we readers, who recognize ourselves in them, will understand our own. These are wise, passionate stories that will not easily be forgotten."

— Erin Mcgraw, author of the New York Times Notable Book, *Lies of the Saints*, along with six other works of fiction, ranging from novels to a collection of very short stories, titled *Joy*

"The nuanced, flawed, and beautiful characters in this collection feel as if they have been cut from real life. Scenes from the book have been marinating in my imagination since my first read. Kevin Fitton exhibits an acute understanding of the longings, loves, and regrets that make each of us human. It's a must-read!"

— Erin Wasinger, author of *A Year of Small Things*

"Kevin Fitton's *Auras* is an elegant and patient meditation on how we persist in the face of loss and separation. Each story examines with precise detail our faults, limitations, and sorrow, but always well-balanced with notes of humor, music, and glory. Fitton is a born storyteller, and *Auras* is a wise and lasting debut."

—Keith Lesmeister, author of the story collection *We Could Have Been Happy Here*

AURAS

Stories

Kevin Fitton

Fomite
Burlington, VT

ISBN-13: 978-1-953236-68-5
Library of Congress Control Number: 2022931418

Fomite
58 Peru Street
Burlington, VT 05401
www.fomitepress.com
08-16-2022

"A Sentimental Person" was first published in *The Saturday Evening Post*, "Crashums" in *The Broad River Review*, "First Night" in *Storgy*, "Man on a Mountain" in *Jabberwock*, "Laura-Jean" in *Limestone*, "Skimming" in *Cottonwood*, "Something Worthy of His Shame" in *The Red Earth Review*, "A Magical Adventures™ Hot Air Balloon Ride" in *Cutleaf*, and "World Upside Down" in *The Hilltop Review*. "Crime and Punishment" was originally published as "Gasoline" in *The Tishman Review*.

Many people helped create this book. I want to express my deep gratitude to my teachers: Heather Sellers, Bret Anthony Johnston, Jill McCorkle, Rachel Pastan, Erin McGraw, and Thisbe Nissen. In all of your different ways, you taught me how to write a story. I also want to thank the many friends and colleagues who took time to read these stories and provide invaluable feedback. Thanks especially to Erin Wasinger and Amber Caron, who read everything, as well as Jessica Danger, April Darcy, Stefani Nellen, Keith Lesmeister, Denton Loving, Victoria Fitton, Rebecca Fitton, Katie Hubert, Ian Bailey, Jana Aupperlee, and Barbara Hauß. Sometimes, writing might seem like a solitary endeavor. Thankfully, for me, it isn't.

Thanks also to Steve Kettman and Sarah Ringler for hosting me at the Wellstone Center in the Redwoods, where I was provided with time and space to finish my manuscript on their beautiful property. Finally, and more than anything, I want to express my gratitude to my daughters, Naomi and Adelaide, and to my wonderful wife, Rebecca, for your incredible patience and support. If it weren't for the three of you, this book could never have come to exist.

CONTENTS

"Desire is no light thing."

—Anne Carson

A Sentimental Person

IT HAD BEEN THREE YEARS since I touched that guitar. Before Lauren died, I played nearly every day—at least picked it up, smelled the earthy aroma of the instrument like mud laced with cinnamon. It surprised me the day I finally took it back out of its case to discover the scent was still there.

There were a few packages of strings in there, too, a capo, and a half-dozen picks, including the green one I caught when Chris Thile threw it into the crowd at the end of a Nickel Creek concert—one of the few good memories from my former life that didn't have Lauren wrapped all around it. Also there were two pieces of paper, folded into squares, with song ideas scratched out in blue ink from a writing session I can barely remember. I used to squirrel away an hour or two for writing whenever I could—a challenge with my responsibilities as a pastor, father and husband. The ideas were half-formed and uninspired, so I threw the papers into the recycling. Forced myself to put them in recycling, I should say. I have a hard time throwing things out. I can admit that.

I have always been a sentimental person. I'm the guy who buys the concert t-shirt and shows up hours early for a baseball game, leaning over the railing and asking for autographs all through batting practice. Some of that memorabilia is in frames or cases, lined up on bookshelves, or adorning the walls of my office at the church and our basement rec room. I was never a pack rat, though. It was after Lauren died, when I started clinging to our possessions.

For example, there was a package of napkins that was about half full when it happened, and with everyone over at the house (my sister, Emily, and Will and Cindy from church), in a couple of days the napkins were nearly used up. When I realized they were almost gone, I panicked. I stuffed the package with the remaining napkins in the back of the pantry. And then there's Lauren's coffee mug, which I won't let anyone wash. It sits on the windowsill behind the sink with a sticky note: "Do not touch." The problem is the finality of it. You put something in the trash, and it's gone forever.

But I was talking about my guitar, a Martin Triple-O Fifteen, built from solid mahogany, front, back, and sides—a guitar which smells to this day like the tree from which it was made.

I don't know what made me finally take it back out, but the moment I held it, I realized how much I missed it—missed the feel of the strings, the rattle of a finger-slap blues riff, the shimmering sound of a D-chord like a chorus of birds.

When I finally removed it from its case (it was more than a thousand days, can you imagine?), the instrument needed a neck adjustment, so I took it to the shop. I didn't have any meetings that afternoon, and my girlfriend, who had been in the picture for several months, was picking the kids up from school.

The relationship was my first in the world of post: post-marriage, post-death, post-everything changing. I had gone on a few dates before I met Helen, but only because Emily kept setting me up. When I met Helen, I was strolling through the Saturday farmer's market. I was kid-free for the weekend, and it was one of the rare days when I actually felt light. In fact, more than once that morning, I double-checked my pockets, because I kept thinking I must have forgotten something. But my keys were there, my wallet, my phone, and my kids were accounted for (an overnight with Will and Cindy, whose kids were the same age as mine).

The sun was out, and the leaves on the trees were that spring-green color, the color that's so fresh looking it makes you think how the tree is a living thing, so full of liquid, when it's punctured, the sap spills out like clear blood. I approached a produce stand that looked especially attractive. Tin buckets held bunches of greens—rainbow chard with bright, neon-colored veins, parsley and spinach, red and green leaf lettuce.

Helen was inspecting some salad greens.

"This is damn beautiful stuff," I said.

"I think veggies are pretty," she said

She was pretty. Not in a bowl-you-over sort of way. But pleasing—pleasant to look at, pleasant to be around. She smiles a lot, has good teeth, rich brown hair with a natural curl, which, if I'm honest, reminds me of Lauren. I had wanted to date women who looked nothing like her—women who would never be confused as a sort of substitute for my dead wife. But you meet whom you meet, and when you're single in middle age, the pickings are pretty slim.

I turned my attention to a display of radishes, purple and pungent, laid out in a row with the stems still attached.

"Veggies is a funny word," I said. "Just listen to it: veggies."

She laughed. I could tell right away she was interested, because she looked at my hand. The ring check. I figured she was younger than me, but still in the range.

"Yup. Single," I said. I had stopped wearing my wedding ring, and instead kept it in a case on my dresser.

"I didn't mean…"

"Yeah, you did." I was surprised at my own self-confidence, but as I said, there was that feeling of lightness.

"Okay, you got me." She smiled that smile again. "God, this is so embarrassing."

I shrugged. "Why? I think you're attractive, and I'm not embarrassed about it."

She turned her head and looked at me sideways.

"You want to blow this vegetable stand and get something to eat?"

"I don't even know your name."

"It's James," I said. I told her to meet me at the fountain in half an hour, and I showed up with a bag full of vegetarian samosas and two cups of coffee, and we sat together on a park bench, and I told all. Two kids, dead wife, pastor. She didn't flinch.

Before Lauren died, I worked a lot. I was obsessive about it really, a trap that's easy for a pastor to fall into. I did care about my church, I will say that. But the thing that drove me was the desire to succeed. Everyone around me—my friends and my peers—could see my work. They could see if the church was growing (or not). They knew if people liked me (or not). I was on display, and that was something I never really came to terms with.

After Lauren, though, I lost my obsession. In the beginning, grieving consumed all of my energy. As time passed, if I'm honest, I started relying on Lauren's death as an excuse. It would have been impossible for the church to demand more of me, and I knew it. And I wouldn't say that I lost my faith, but I lost my certainty. Part of me wanted to keep running just as hard as before, but how does a person run full steam ahead when he isn't sure where he's going?

While I waited for the repair tech to finish the tune-up, I saw an advertisement for a blues guitar class, and I signed up right then and there. People were always encouraging me to do things: go on trips, start dating, take a class. They were worried that I was like a car, and if I sat still too long, I would stop running. It's shit, really, the way people try to cut your grief short. That's my biggest piece of advice if someone in your life goes through this kind of loss. Sit with them and let them grieve. They're going to hurt—that's not something you can change—and it's going to take longer than you think it should. Grief isn't water soluble; it doesn't wash away.

But I was talking about my blues guitar class. Our teacher, Pinkerton Shaw, white and Midwestern like me, played the Delta Blues with the soul of a sharecropper. Five of us sat together in the living room of his house in an artsy neighborhood along the Grand River, and Pinky (the perfect bluesman's name, right?) taught us theory, the blues box, the pentatonic scale, and a handful of different grooves. There's no point in false modesty, so I'll just go ahead and say that I was the best player in the group—except for Pinky, of course.

I started hanging around after class, sharing a beer, and listening to his stories from Berklee (where he crossed paths with John Mayer and Diana Krall—how's that for a brush with fame?) and from life on the road.

I didn't tell him about Lauren right off. He knew I had two kids and that I was dating. Pinky was married, and they had a newborn, which is why he'd given up the touring life, bought a house back in his hometown, and filled it with second-hand furniture.

I told him that I loved bottleneck blues, and he offered to teach me how to play slide, and I started staying later and later after class.

"Man, you could really be a player," he said one night. It was summer in Michigan, and the sun was taking forever to set. At ten o'clock, the last gasps of grey light still refused to falter. Night crept up on us, and we didn't turn the lights on, even when it was almost dark.

I leaned my guitar against the wall and settled into my chair.

"Did you ever think about pursuing your music?" he asked.

"Not really. I married young, started down another path."

He was wearing a dark grey button-up with the sleeves rolled up to the elbows, and even in the near dark, I could see the blue vein running down the center of his underarm.

"Can I ask what happened?" he asked.

"You just did."

He smiled and played a riff.

"My wife died three years ago. It was a stroke. One day she was there, and then she was gone."

"Oh, shit. I'm sorry."

"It was terrible, but it's getting better. It's starting to get better."

"I don't know what to say," he said.

I shrugged.

I'll say this for Pinky. I know he was uncomfortable. But he didn't look away or bring up some story of loss he'd experienced. He said, "I'm really sorry," and he looked me in the eyes.

I mentioned before that I was feeling uncertain about my relationship with Helen. There were plenty of things I liked about her. I was attracted to her. She was stubbornly idealistic, a quality I admired. And she had won over my kids, Danny and Ruth—my two preteens—which is no small feat.

But then there were things that bothered me. Like, for example, she would offer to watch the kids, and then she was annoyed when I didn't come home right after class. She didn't really care that I was late (she was a night owl and never went to bed early). It was jealousy. She was jealous of Pinky, and she was threatened by my history with Lauren. She never said so, but I could tell. I could tell by the way she turned quiet when the kids talked about their mom. I could tell by the way she stole glances at Lauren's coffee mug on the windowsill while she did the dishes.

And then there were the petty things—her laugh, for example. She had a laugh like a two-stroke engine: hick, hick—hick, hick. And I know this is going to sound terribly superficial, but she had trouble with her skin. Near-constant breakouts on her chin and forehead, which she smothered with makeup, theorizing that it was caused by chocolate (while she ate chocolate) or by drinking alcohol (while holding a glass of wine).

What bothered me is that she didn't do anything about it. She didn't go to the dermatologist or change her diet. She didn't even wash her face before bed, which is me admitting that she sometimes stayed over.

One day that summer, Helen and I took a trip to Lake Michigan. We walked the Saugatuck Dunes, a hilly forest of beach grass, oaks, and white pines, ending in a strip of white sand at the water's edge. Then we headed into town, built on the mouth of the Kalamazoo River, a perfect harbor for boaters. We held hands as we walked, watching the sunlight reflecting on the water and the rows of aluminum masts, rocking in the gentle waves.

"Let's play a game," she said. "We walk two blocks this way, turn right, and then we eat dinner at the first restaurant we see."

"I know a good place," I said.

"No, that's too easy." She turned to face me.

"But it's so arbitrary," I said.

She kept pushing, and I decided to go along with it. And, of course, she was right. Dinner was great.

The first song Pinky and I performed together was at church. Pinky and his wife, Jayna, started coming on Sunday mornings with their baby. They were the type that grew up in church, drifted away during college, but when they had a child, started talking about going back. And then I came along.

We worked up a version of the old song, "Nothing but the Blood," a hymn with the heart of a spiritual with its call and response. "What can wash away my sin? *Nothing but the blood of Jesus.* What can make me whole again? *Nothing but the blood of Jesus.*" You get the idea. There's nothing complicated about it, and that's the point.

I sang lead. Pinky added background vocals and some killer fills on guitar. The song leaves some breathing room between lines, and we stretched out the space between chorus and verse so Pinky could play the way he does, his fingers flying across the neck of his guitar, both frenetic and effortless.

We made it into a sort of theme and variation, adding layers of complexity with each verse, and even playing with the melody. The best way to handle repetition is to treat the whole thing like a suggestion. Start here, start here, the music says. But it doesn't tell you were to go. It's up to you to give it soul, build it up until it soars. And it did. It took off, mostly because Pinky is so damn good. Once we got going, it sounded like there were four of us up there playing, and I can assure you, I was only carrying one part. We repeated the last chorus three times and then, finally, ended the song. Pinky hit one last chord and let it ring. After a moment's hesitation, the church let go with applause.

The amazing thing about music is that it can become a sort of bridge between the performer and the audience, a shared experience. Of course, not everyone feels it. Maybe ten percent, fifteen percent. Helen wasn't one of them. "You sing really well." It was the only compliment Helen could manage, when she wasn't criticizing Pinky's outfit (he wore all black), or his voice (his vocals are solid but nasal and pinched). I tried to explain the theme-and-variations thing but didn't get anywhere.

At this point, I seriously considered breaking up with her. Sometimes, it was like we were speaking in translation. There was something fundamental about me that she didn't under-stand. But I was afraid of letting go (see napkins, see coffee mug); she cut the loneliness in my life like cream to coffee. And then there was the kids.

I mentioned before that she won over my children. This didn't just happen. Danny, in particular, resisted her. One

day—it must have been around six weeks into our relationship—Helen was talking with Danny, and he was agitated.
It was typical stuff. We planned to hike to a little lake nearby,
and Danny didn't want to go. Helen got down on her knees to
talk with him, and Danny reared back and hit her with both
hands square in her shoulders.

I didn't see it happen, but I saw the immediate aftermath—
the look of anger on Danny's face and shock on Helen's. But
she didn't yell at him or even turn away; she stayed right down
there with him, looking him in the eyes. She said, "I bet sometimes you just want to hit someone, don't you? It isn't fair, is it?"

Danny didn't say anything, but later, when we were walking back from our swim, he took her hand. It was a turning
point for all of us. There were still moments of resistance, but
she just kept bearing with them. Even more than her natural
optimism, it was her most admirable quality.

Pinky's blues class ended, but we kept meeting on Wednesday
nights. I started bringing song lyrics (usually in bits and
pieces), and Pinky came up with the music. When he worked
on a song, he seemed to draw from a bottomless store of
chord progressions, melodies, and countermelodies, as if he
had tapped into flowing water deep underground. We ended
up with some great sounding stuff, even though I wasn't holding up my end of the bargain. My lyrics were stiff. I didn't

recognize it at the time, but I was a man poking at my feelings with a stick. I wrote a song about a homeless man, a troubled marriage, and one about a whale hunt. The song about whales was probably the best, or at least that's what Jayna said. Pinky didn't come out and say it, but I could tell he wasn't satisfied. He was waiting.

School was now underway again, and Helen spent most evenings at our house, heading straight from work to pick up Danny from soccer or Ruth from lacrosse. She was a savior for our family. I cooked dinner while she supervised homework, scrubbed pots and pans, and packed lunches. We were a solid team. And this, I started to remind myself, was life. Life was raising children, going to meetings, and making the best we can out of the moments in between, the little shafts of light.

It was October by the time we managed a real date night, our first since the trip to Saugatuck. She got ready at her own place, and I picked her up, wearing a new shirt and a dash of cologne.

"What do they call this?" I asked.

"A date?" she said.

"Romance," I said. "That's the word."

I could give you the whole blow-by-blow, the way the evening unfolded, or I could simply say that I was a man divided, a split personality—infatuated with this beautiful woman, unspeakably grateful that she was helping put my family back together, and, at the same time, guilty as hell that I was moving on from Lauren. So I did what any reasonable person would do in my situation: I drank. A lot.

We went to a new brewery, which gave me a decent excuse for trying a number of beers. I started with a few samples and then ordered my first pint, and then another. Helen offered to drive.

Soon I could think of only one thing: sex. I've already admitted that we slept together, but I should clarify that, as a pastor, this was against the rules. And I know that it's an excuse, but when your wife has died and you've gone years without sex, the hunger is insatiable.

We were seated at a high top, and each time I went to the bathroom, the step down to the floor seemed to grow. I passed Helen on my way, kissed her neck, and stared at the stone tiled wall in the bathroom while I peed. Then I sauntered back to the table.

"Want to blow this vegetable stand," I said, finally.

"Sure."

"Your place."

On the drive, she turned quiet. As soon as we entered her house, she held up her hand—literally held up her hand like a traffic cop—and said, "James, what do you want from me?"

"What do you mean?"

"You know exactly what I mean."

There were tears in her eyes. She was standing straight as a pin.

"You tell me you care about me, but then you turn around and act like a jerk. You're fine with me tutoring your kids, having sex with me." She stopped. The word sex hung in the air, the long whispering esses.

I was in no condition to talk about it or drive myself home. She made me a coffee and said she would take me home when I sobered up. I turned on the television, so we didn't have to talk. And, honestly, we never really circled back to the conversation. I told her I was sorry and that was it.

Pinky and I decided to play an open mic at a coffee shop in the warehouse district. All we needed was one song, so I kept writing. I once heard Wynton Marsalis describe how he would write for hours and sometimes keep nothing more than a line or a phrase. And so I kept working, until I finally had something.

Not long before Lauren died, the PTA brought a magician to our kids' school for a fundraiser. The show was in the auditorium with a reception in the cafeteria, where they served appetizers and punch in plastic stemware.

On the way to the event, Lauren and I were arguing about something. We were running late and stressed, and I'm sure we were both aggravated, but the kicker is that I remember thinking during the magic show, "I wish this guy would make my wife disappear." I didn't really mean it, but the thought ran through my head, and then, in a matter of weeks, she was gone. Really gone.

Anyway, this is what the song is about: magic tricks and making things disappear and then wishing they would come back. About regret and death and how it is completely and utterly relentless. It wasn't the greatest song in the world, but it was a big improvement from my other stuff, and at least it was honest.

Helen came to the open mic. We hadn't exactly returned to normal, but it seemed like we were moving in that direction. Pinky and I were pretty early in the schedule, and there weren't many people in the room when we played our song, which was disappointing after all the work we put into it. The host called us to the front, and we waded through tables and chairs heading toward the makeshift stage, framed by the two speakers, mounted on those flimsy plastic floor stands. There was seating for about two dozen people at eight or nine tables, and the place was half full. We plugged in, played the song, and then it was over. A few people seemed really into it, nodding their heads and tapping on the table to keep time. Mostly, the experience was anticlimactic. We played our song, people clapped, and we sat down.

Helen bent over and whispered in my ear. "That was really good." She locked eyes with me, and I knew she meant it.

What I never expected was that, after two more acts (another singer-songwriter and a poet), the host called the next performer to the stage, and it was someone I never expected. It was Helen.

Before saying anything else, I should also mention that the place was now packed. Late arrivers filled the open tables, and some were even standing around the edges, leaning against the brick walls. If she was intimidated, she didn't show it. When her name was called, Helen took a deep breath and marched to the stage, Pinky in tow. (They'd spent two weeks working on it; he filled me in later.)

They covered the U2 song, "Where the Streets Have No Name," and it says something right there that she knew enough to pick a classic and a song that worked well with her voice. She sang on key, even when the melody jumped to a different range, but what was most striking was the way she rounded her phrases, instead of simply sitting on the notes. She didn't have a big voice, but it was cool, with a little bit of grit, a little bit of texture. And, of course, Pinky knocked it out of the park.

It was the performance of the night, and, as far as I was concerned, it came out of nowhere. After nine months of dating, I should have known. But here I was, completely shocked at what had just taken place.

There's a lot more I could say about how things ended between us, but I'm trying to stick to the parts that really matter. And I think it's enough to say that she was really gracious, and that I learned something about how self-absorbed I was. I should also add that she still regularly visits the kids, and not only because she understands how difficult it would be for them to lose another mother figure. She really cares about them and makes time for them, even though it's been a year since she broke it off.

If I sound nostalgic, I might not be getting my point across. I don't miss dating Helen; we weren't a good match. It isn't even quite right to say that I have regrets. That's not it, either. Not exactly. I wish I had treated her better, and I'm sorry for that, but I don't wish things had happened any differently. I've apologized, and she doesn't need anything else from me. She's a lot stronger than I realized.

I've said before that this kind of grieving doesn't ever end. Lauren's death changed me in ways that are permanent. But today, finally, I put that coffee mug in the dishwasher and ran it through. And then I put it back into the cabinet with the others.

As for Pinky and me, we're still getting together. Still working, still playing. My writing is getting better, little by little, though I'm still trying to write the song that answers the question I don't know how to ask.

A Magical Adventures™ Hot Air Balloon Ride

THE FAIRGROUNDS IN BATTLE CREEK were soft from an overnight shower. Tires left impressions where trucks had driven over the field. Nora could see where a vehicle had gotten stuck in a ditch, spinning its wheels and opening a gash in the earth. Her shoes were little more than slippers. She walked carefully, leaping over puddles. On more than one occasion, though, she misjudged the terrain and landed in a soft spot, sinking into a pool of dirty water. More than likely, her shoes would be ruined.

Nora was meeting her stepdaughter, Chelsea, at the Ferris wheel. Chelsea was a rising junior at Michigan State and was staying in East Lansing for the summer. She had landed an internship working for a political campaign, and it was an all-consuming job. Except for one weekend in June, she hadn't had the opportunity to visit her home in suburban

Detroit, even though it was only an hour's drive. Chelsea didn't know that Nora and David, her father, separated two weeks ago.

Originally, Nora had bought the tickets for her and David. Things had been rough for a while, but she hadn't expected that it would disintegrate to this extent, where they couldn't spend fifteen minutes together without arguing. There was no way she was going to go on a hot air balloon ride with him, stuck together in a basket thousands of feet in the air. When Nora invited Chelsea, she made an excuse for her father, claiming he had to work. Initially, not telling Chelsea about the separation felt like the right decision. It was wise, waiting to see if they're able to work things out. But the omission was turning into a lie.

Chelsea hadn't exactly jumped at the opportunity. When she agreed, it felt like a concession to the parent who sent extra money for work clothes and going out with friends. Nora wasn't Chelsea's mother, but she had been married to David for over a decade and had known Chelsea since she was seven. She could tell when something was wrong. There was a timbre in her stepdaughter's voice, high pitched and uncertain, that betrayed when she wasn't telling the truth.

"Are you sure?" Nora had asked.

"Yes. Definitely. It sounds fun." Her voice squeaked. She was lying.

The festivities included an air show and a small carnival. It was early evening, and the carnival had yet to pick up. Rides were running, but most of the seats were unoccupied, the benches swinging without passengers. A biplane flew overhead, dipping and diving, spouting trails of smoke. The sun burned in the blue sky, floating between clouds. It was impossible to look into the sky. She tried, but even with sunglasses, her vision blurred with tears. Although it had rained, the humidity hadn't broken, and she was sweating.

Several balloon teams were already in the field, pick-up trucks and covered trailers spaced out on the muddy lawn. Balloons and baskets waited in the stifling heat of the metal trailers.

Nora had obsessed over balloons for the past few months, starting with a friend's videos and pictures on Facebook. She must have watched dozens of launch videos on YouTube. She found the whole thing fascinating.

It starts with a basket lying prone on its side with the material of the balloon stretched out over the grass like a dead man. The pilot starts the fan, and the thing stirs to life. When the balloon is filled with air, the fan is replaced with the burner. The burner roars, shooting flame. Until, finally, it happens: the balloon rises. Slowly, it pivots away from the earth, until the balloon and basket are standing upright. Full of energy, the balloon tugs at its tethers, eager to fly. And this was all before the launch even took place, which might be the greatest moment of all—the big, beautiful apparatus released from the ground and forging its way into the sky.

It was such a marvelous contradiction, this thing that was machine and not machine, playful and also serious, majestic and at the same time, incredibly fragile. If you thought about it, the whole thing was crazy, traveling thousands of feet into the air in a basket, which hangs from a balloon that is powered by an open flame. And yet the flight is serene.

Nora had a tendency to obsess. A couple of years before, it was speech recognition software. A friend at work mentioned how far the technology had come, how she used it for journal entries and voice memos. Immediately, Nora started researching the latest products, buying a premium package within a couple of days. She installed the software on her laptop and spent hours talking into the microphone, watching her thoughts appear as words on the screen. After the speech recognition software, it was the hybrid mattress, which did help them sleep better, until David moved to the guest bedroom and then to a hotel.

Now it was hot air balloons.

Chelsea was leaning against a picnic table when Nora found her. She was little, barely five feet and cute as a button. Nora was five-ten. And, of course, that was tall, but most of the time, she felt normal-tall. Around Chelsea, she felt like a giant. When they embraced, Chelsea's head tucked into Nora's shoulder, a maneuver that kept Chelsea's face from landing in her stepmom's breasts.

Chelsea was smart enough to wear boots and was unconcerned with the mud. She led the way as they searched for their launch site, Nora following along in her silly flats. The company was called Magical Adventures™ with a logo of a balloon falling over a horizon like a setting sun. Nora was a graphic artist by trade. She worked for a large credit union, designing publications and web content, and she was fussy about logos. This one was amateurish. It was too busy, and the name was all wrong. It made her think of Disney World, and she didn't want fantasy. She wanted something real. She wanted to hear the flame burn—that crash of sound. She wanted to feel the sway of the basket as it jumped away from the ground, a pit opening up in her stomach.

The pilot, Eric, was sitting in his truck with the doors hanging open. The trailer was open, too, and they could see the basket and the balloon fabric, overflowing its bag. Seeing it in-person, she was struck by the fact that it was, in fact, a giant woven basket—that someone had woven these huge reeds, an inch in diameter, through spokes the size of saplings, making a basket that was big enough and strong enough to carry three full-grown adults into the sky.

They signed their release forms, using the trailer as a

writing surface. A cloud covered the sun, providing temporary relief from the heat.

"I'm glad you were able to come," Nora said. "Did you skip out early?"

"Well, when they aren't paying you…"

They *were* paying Chelsea for data entry and social media stuff, but canvassing and stuffing envelopes was voluntary. She was more worn out than Nora had anticipated and seemed irritated. The mismatched women, Nora a full head taller, leaned back against the trailer and watched the biplane complete its routine. It turned a reverse somersault, a loop-de-loop worthy of a roller coaster.

Soon Eric and his two-man crew were preparing to fly. They lifted the basket out of the trailer and removed the balloon from its bag. Nora and Chelsea jumped in to help, each grabbing an edge of the heavy nylon, working to unfurl the balloon. Eric, Nora noticed, was keeping an eye on Chelsea. It happened all the time—men looking at her stepdaughter. At least Eric was discreet.

As it filled with air, Nora circled the balloon. It was so strange seeing the giant balloon up close, hearing the blast of the burner, watching the balloon slowly rise. She was lost in the moment, taking video with her phone, when she heard Eric calling.

Chelsea was climbing into the basket when Nora arrived. Eric gave Chelsea a hand, although she didn't need it. He turned his attention to the balloon when Nora approached, assuming she could manage on her own.

Finally, they were standing in the basket, she and Chelsea and Eric, the balloon a giant cavern above them. The colors were crisp: linen white, citrus orange, berry blue. The basket was never completely still. It was a boat in the harbor, rocking in place.

A crowd had grown. Groups of people were walking through the field, looking at the balloons and chatting with the pilots. A few spectators gathered when Eric started the fan, and more came when he lit the burner. By the time they were ready to launch—the first balloon of the evening!—a crowd of about thirty stood around them on the matted grass. The huge balloon cast a shadow over the onlookers.

Chelsea had this particular look on her face, the look she got when she discovered some new aspect of the world. When they walked to the edge of the Grand Canyon and saw the unbelievable distances, down to the Colorado River at the bottom of the gorge, to the rim on the opposite side. When, on the same trip, Old Faithful erupted right on schedule, and then when a herd of buffalo crossed the road in front of them, just a few feet from their car. And then there were the cultural experiences, when she discovered the Beatles and Michael Jackson, and the movies: *Shawshank*, *Caddyshack*, *Star Wars*. It was that same look: *This exists? This is possible?*

It took Nora a moment before she realized that they were moving. The basket quaked. She grabbed onto the rim and saw that the ground was retreating. She looked all around, taking it in—the launch team leaning against the big truck, watching; the inside of the balloon, giant above her head; and then, finally, the group of spectators in an unkempt semi-circle, which was when she thought she saw David in the back of the crowd. She was just about to tell Chelsea when she realized that it wasn't him, after all, just a man of a similar height and build, wearing a Tigers hat like the one David often wore.

She had invited him over the day before, hoping they could have lunch, spend time together, and not argue. She hid the divorce papers in the bottom drawer of her dresser, underneath her folded jeans.

When he arrived, she handed him a beer. He used a bottle opener that he kept stuck to the fridge and set the cap on the counter. There was already a patch of sweat in the middle of his shirt, and he started right in on his latest talking-point: counseling. With David, everything was a negotiation. He was a high school debate champion turned lawyer, and she knew all of his tactics. Raising the ask and negotiating back down, clouding the primary issue with side issues, and, most relevant to their separation, persisting in making the same point, over and over and over.

She threw away the cap and leaned back against the countertop. On the one hand, she felt as if they *should* go to counseling. She wanted to be able to say that she tried everything. And who knew? Maybe a counselor would be able to somehow, magically, heal the rift that had opened up between them—between the wife who wanted to have a baby and the husband who didn't. At this point, though, reconciliation was hard to imagine. She was forty-two years old, and even if David changed his mind, it was probably too late—too late to get pregnant and too late to forgive him for dragging his feet. For that matter, she didn't think she could forgive herself for letting it happen, for failing to draw the line when she was in her thirties and there was still time.

She placed her palms against the counter and felt the cool in the granite, obstinate against the humidity. David was saying that the problem with their marriage was a lack of effort.

"You always make me out to be the problem," she said.

"I didn't say you were the problem. I said that *we* aren't trying hard enough."

"That's hilarious," she said.

David kept going. He finished his speech and then cocked his head. He was waiting for her gambit, in order to properly measure his counterattack.

"You think everything can be solved by negotiation," she said, "but this isn't a debate, David. This isn't something you can talk your way around."

"I want to work on things. I'm talking about engaging in a process, Nora."

"This is why we can't go on the balloon ride together, because we'll just argue the whole time."

David went to mow the lawn, and she advanced the laundry. When she returned to the kitchen, she could see him working outside. He had taken off his shirt, revealing his white skin and shallow chest. She had touched that body so many times, and yet, at the moment, it felt like a distant memory.

She rinsed out an insulated water bottle and filled it with ice water. Then she walked out to the deck and put the water bottle in the slatted shade of the balusters, pointing it out to David with a wave. He kept mowing, circling the backyard, turning right again and again and again. His skin looked slippery, his jeans soaked.

When she and David first started dating, Chelsea was seven. They would sit on the deck with glasses of wine, and Chelsea would play in the water, yelling "Look at me!" And they would yell, "We see you!"

One time, in a moment of inspiration, David ran down the steps and vaulted into the spray. He grabbed Chelsea and hung her upside down over the sprinkler, the girl laughing hysterically. Then, as he set her down, he slipped and fell into a puddle. Grass clippings stuck to his face and hair. His jeans and shirt clung to his skin. Nora laughed so hard. He was a single father who never seemed overwhelmed by the difficulty of his situation. David rarely talked about Elizabeth, his ex, and whenever Nora questioned him, wondering how he could be so tolerant, he would say: "It's worse for her. Believe me."

The balloon rose, and they could soon see the whole fairground. There were another half-dozen balloons, their crews in various stages of preparation, readying to fly. There were people on the Ferris wheel, the top of which they were about to eclipse. Across the street, strip malls and big box stores flattened into two-dimensional squares and rectangles. Things on the ground, its people and trees and buildings, were shrinking, even as the earth stretched out before her, the horizon growing wider and wider. The breeze was light, and the only way to tell they were moving was the balloon's shadow skipping across the ground below.

"God," she said.

"Holy shit," Chelsea said.

They were riding an invisible current.

"Three thousand feet," Eric said. "A good height."

She was thinking about David. From this height, even her anger felt small and distant. For months now, she had been thinking about her marriage as if it had been a mistake, as if David was nothing but a wrong turn. But now, with her arm around Chelsea, she admitted to herself that, given the choice, she would do it all over again.

For fifteen minutes, they drifted along, looking down at the world: towns, rivers, highways. Eric explained how he could control the path of the balloon by rising or sinking into different currents.

"It's nothing like steering," he said, "but we have our tricks."

When Eric stopped talking, though, she noticed that Chelsea was quiet. Her eyes were red.

"What's wrong?" she asked.

Chelsea didn't respond right away. Eric fired the torch, and, for a moment, there was nothing but the sound of gas exploding into flame. There was a burst of heat. She felt it in her eyes and neck. When the burn was over, the world was still.

"I know something's going on with you and Dad," she said.

Nora stared into the distance. Assuming the wind was heading straight east, they would be heading toward Ann Arbor or Ypsilanti, and beyond that Detroit and Lake St. Clair.

"We're separated," she said.

"Why didn't you tell me?"

The idea had been to protect her, but now that she was asked to defend the decision, she realized it was absurd. The real reason, the naked truth, was that she didn't want to face her own greatest fear: that divorcing David would mean losing Chelsea. David was her father, the one person who had always been, and would always be, in her life. What if Elizabeth finally got her act together? Nora'd heard stories of young adults becoming fascinated with their birth mothers and pushing away the women who had stepped in to raise them, who had cleaned up the spills and the vomit, socked away money into a college savings account, monitored social media accounts, laid down the law when necessary. The absent mother didn't have to fight the battles, never had to be the enforcer.

"I don't know," Nora said, but Chelsea turned away, back to the west, where they had come from. This was when Nora noticed the bank of dark clouds rolling in, quickly overtaking them.

"I don't like the look of that," Eric said.

He picked up his CB and called the team back on the ground.

"We're worried about weather up here," he said. "Dark clouds and it feels like the temperature's dropping." He was wearing a baseball hat with the Magical Adventures™ logo, and he took it off for a moment, combed his hair with his fingers, and slid it back onto his head.

The wind was definitely stronger; goose bumps were spreading across Nora's arms. There was nothing on the radar, though; the closest visible storm was over eastern Wisconsin, three hundred miles away.

"I'm not taking any chances." Eric turned his attention to captaining the balloon, but before he did, he again looked at Chelsea, his eyes scrolling over her body. It was getting darker, but Nora could still see his eyes.

He released air through an opening in the top of the balloon and announced that they were descending, though the change wasn't obvious. They continued their course through the sky, adrift in the heavens.

Eric chose this time to start a conversation. Probably, he was trying to project calm. He asked what they thought about their first balloon ride.

"It's pretty great," Nora said. "So far."

Eric asked Chelsea if she was a college student.

She explained her status: rising junior, summer internship, plans to become a political consultant.

"That's interesting," Eric said, and he launched into a story about a friend of his who worked for the former Democratic governor and current Republican speaker of the house. "It isn't about ideology. It's about getting things done," he added.

"Definitely," Chelsea agreed.

Nora was annoyed, first of all, that Eric was preaching at Chelsea about politics. But even more so, she felt left out. It was pathetic, but she was jealous. She was about to be a single woman, and this middle-age man was heaping all of his attention on her twenty-year-old daughter. She turned away from the conversation and looked over the edge of the basket. They were, in fact, losing altitude. The tops of the tallest trees were now just a couple hundred feet below them.

"I hate to interrupt," she said.

Eric checked his altimeter and then fired the burner. He picked up the CB. "Looking for a landing spot," he said.

The crew was worried about weather now, too. There still wasn't anything on the radar, but the barometric pressure was dropping.

"Hey, did you feel that?" Chelsea asked.

A light rain started. First, it was just a few drops. Sporadic raindrops became a sprinkle, and then it was raining, a gentle shower that coated their necks and arms. Nora asked Eric if the rain was a problem.

"It's not great, but we have an experienced team. We'll deal with it." Again, he picked up the radio and gave their position.

Nora wrapped her arm around Chelsea, rubbing her shoulder. They were both shivering.

The team identified a landing spot, a hay field up ahead. But it had turned dark. The setting sun was buried behind a bank of dark clouds, rain was falling, and it was difficult to see what was happening beneath them. They would have to rely on the guidance from the crew driver below and make a nearly blind landing.

"You've done this before?" Nora asked. In reply, Eric stoked the burner, a long blast, to check their progress. He was managing their descent, but there was another consequence to the burn: the flame, a giant torch, lit up the world around them. And for just a moment she could see it all—a road at their left, a big open field ahead, but right before the field, a row of trees, their leaves flashing white in the surge of light. She didn't think they were high enough.

"Look!" she shouted.

The three of them ducked inside the basket, bracing as they crashed through a tree. She heard twigs breaking—scraping and snapping—but the balloon didn't stop. The basket tipped, leaning, while the balloon surged ahead of them, but then it broke free and, like a pendulum, swung back to center—the weight of the passengers serving as ballast.

"Everyone okay?" Eric asked.

Chelsea seemed startled, her palms pressed against the bottom of the basket. Nora, though, wanted to see what was happening. Even while it was still rocking, she grabbed the edge of the basket and pulled herself to her feet. They were fifty feet high, if that, and dropping fast.

She gripped the basket with one hand, held onto Chelsea with the other, and waited.

Eric lit the burner again, another flash of light. They were about to land in the middle of the clearing. The ground was rushing past them like a river. She could sense it, the power of all that momentum.

The impact sent Nora flying. She was thrown into the basket, headfirst. She struck the crown of her head, but before she was able to consider her injuries, she was thrown again, utterly compelled by the force of the collision. This time, she landed against Chelsea. They were a tangle of limbs.

The basket was still moving, but now she heard voices. The landing team had caught them. Eventually, the balloon stopped. Eric leaped to his feet, releasing air from the vent, allowing the balloon to settle to the ground.

There was pain in her head and neck, but it was muted by adrenaline. Chelsea was moaning.

"Are you okay?" she asked.

The landing crew repeated Nora's question. "Are you okay? Is everyone okay?"

"I think…" Chelsea said.

Nora climbed out of the basket. With help, Chelsea made it too, falling into the arms of the landing team.

Nora was dizzy, and she sat on the ground next to the basket with Chelsea. The rain had stopped. She heard one of the crew members tell Eric, "You're one lucky son of a bitch." It wasn't a graceful landing by any stretch, but it could have been a lot worse.

Both of the crew's vehicles were running, their head-lights casting a spray of light over the scene, drawing long shadows with sharp edges. For a few minutes, they watched as the crew members forced the remaining air out of the balloon. Nora was exhausted, but she wanted to get Chelsea out of the cold.

"Okay, girl," she said. "Let's get you someplace warm."

"I'm okay. For real."

Nora helped Chelsea to her feet. Hunching down, she put her arm around Chelsea's middle, the two of them lumbering toward the trucks like an awkward, four-legged animal, coping with the uneven ground as best they could.

"Look at my shoes," Nora said. She laughed. They were drenched in mud and completely destroyed.

They were ten feet from the truck when Chelsea stopped. "I'm so dizzy," she said.

Nora was holding her upright, and she could tell that Chelsea was done walking. Nora knelt down, laced one hand under her step-daughter's knees, one under her back, and picked her up.

As little as Chelsea was, she was still an adult woman, and it was all Nora could do to hold on to her. Nora leaned back, centering the weight on her hips, moving one step at a time. She only made it a few steps when she heard a member of the landing team running toward them, shouting, "Wait, let me help. You're going to hurt yourself."

Nora's legs trembled, and she practically dropped Chelsea as she set her down. In the end, it was Jeff, one of the crew members, who carried Chelsea the rest of the way and placed her in the back seat of the truck.

Twice, Jeff asked Chelsea if she was okay, and Chelsea insisted she was fine.

"I'm dizzy," she said, "but otherwise I feel okay." Then Jeff closed the door and went back to help pack the balloon and basket.

Nora sat on the bumper for a few minutes and watched the men work, watched them feeding the fabric into its bag, like a snake crawling into a hole. It was cold and wet, and she stuck her hands in her pockets. They were calling out to one another, giving directions. That was when it struck her: it was over. Tears welled up in her eyes, gratitude overflowing. Later, she would be angry. She would tell her friends the story and the anger would well up, and she would say that she was thinking about suing their asses off. But not now.

Nora settled into her seat, and Chelsea lay her head in her lap. There was a kink in her neck. In the morning, she would be sore all over; she could already tell. She would be angry, too. But, at least for the moment, as she stroked Chelsea's head with the tips of her fingers, she felt something else. Bliss.

She had heard mothers talk about how, after labor and childbirth were over, the newborn laid on their chest, the agony melted away. They had passed through the storm. They were beaten and bruised. But none of that mattered.

"Sweet, sweet girl," she said. And she leaned over and kissed her bare arm, which was still cool and wet.

"Mom," Chelsea said, burrowing into her lap.

The first time Chelsea called her Mom was more than a month after she and David were married. It took all of Nora's restraint just to hope it would come naturally. And then, one day, finally, she said it: "Mom, what is there for breakfast?" The smallest thing, such a little word.

Man on a Mountain

Outside, snow fell. The weathermen had been talking about the storm for a couple of days. Benjamin hadn't believed it. It seemed like it happened every year—the warnings of a snowstorm that never materialized. It had been decades since there was a major snowfall. It was Tennessee, after all. Even in the mountains, they only got a couple of inches per winter.

He realized he should stand, walk to the window, and assess the situation, since he would soon need to travel the eighteen miles down out of the mountains to the hospital in Knoxville. But he didn't want to stand, and he didn't really want to know about the drifts of snow piling up outside like sand dunes forming mountains and valleys in the tunneling wind.

He groaned, pressed down against the arms of his chair and shifted his weight. When his kidneys had started to fail, his body began retaining fluid, and that was on top of the forty or fifty pounds he already needed to lose.

He inspected his fingernails. Lately, he'd obsessed over his nails, which had brittled and turned the pale yellow color of diluted urine. He felt for cracks, tried to decide if the color was clearing. At the moment, he was pretty sure it was getting worse. It had been three days since his last dialysis appointment, and he could already feel the depletion in his body like a summer stream exhausted to a trickle.

Standing had become an event. First, he prepared himself. Then he grabbed the arms of his recliner, his hands stretched out like talons. He rocked, rocked again, and pushed, creating just enough momentum to hoist his giant mound of a torso over his wobbly legs. It was the sort of thing even a year ago that he would watch older men do and think how pathetic it was when life came to this. He had just turned sixty-two, and on the one hand, he could feel the clock ticking, but on the other, his youth felt incredibly near, as if it were stored somewhere in his crowded attic. He could remember what it felt like to drag a shot deer out of the woods—the strain in his shoulders and back, the burning in his quads.

He remembered one buck, in particular. His daughter, Jo, was with him when he shot it. It was her first hunt—she was eight or nine at the time. After the kill, he field dressed the animal. Jo watched as he cut the deer open with his knife. At first, it seemed like she would be okay. But then she turned away.

"Ew, gross," she said. She hid behind a tree while he finished.

He tied his rope to the deer's antlers and trudged out of the woods. It was a big deer, and it was an effort to haul. The day was warming, and he was soaked with sweat by the time they made it back to the truck.

Benjamin shuffled over the carpet, past the coffee table, which was piled with dirty bowls and spoons, mugs still half full of coffee. He walked past the ragged couch where he slept beneath the one quilt Margie had sewn, yellow and blue, faded, and yawning open at the seams. She had sewn the quilt twenty years ago, the last time they'd had a storm like the one they were having now. Margie was the sort of person who didn't know how to sit still. She would move all day, and when she did finally sit down, she was guaranteed to pull out her knitting or start cutting coupons. When that storm struck, and she knew she wasn't going anywhere, she started piling fabric on the floor.

Thank goodness he'd had the foresight months ago to move his clothes down to the hunting room on the first floor. When he reached the hallway and was about to enter the room, he paused and leaned against the doorframe. The head of the buck (the same buck he'd shot on Jo's first hunting trip) was there, mounted, preserved, and staring back at him.

"What do you want?" He felt dizzy and gripped the door frame. The deer's glass eyes looked like black pearls. "Now I'm talking to myself."

He entered the room and began the exhausting work of dressing. He pinched the waist of his sweat pants with his swollen fingers and wriggled his pajama bottoms to the ground. His jeans, even with their elastic waist, were the hard part. Several times he stopped to rest, his eyes drawn to a row of fishing lures lined up on top of the gun cabinet—the bright lures in sunflower yellows and pollen oranges, rich lavenders and crab apple reds. Benjamin worked in thirty-second shifts, leaning against his plywood desk, until he was finally able with one last tug to draw his pants up to his waist. Then it was on to the next project: buttoning his shirt.

Despite the frustrations that came with dressing, this room was his oxygen. It was a reminder of the things in life for which he was fighting: his time in the woods and his daughter. He had, to this end, added two framed photographs of his daughter Jo, now thirty-five years old and living in San Bernadino, California, to his desk. One of the photographs was recent, of Jo and her current boyfriend, a black man named Darren. At least, Darren was in the original photograph. Benjamin cut him out to fit the frame, leaving only his arm and a bit of his leg. The other picture was Jo's senior photo, taken in front of an old maple tree behind the house, when her mother was still alive.

Life. It was here in this room—this musty old room with its smells of rust, and mildew, and pine, where Doctor Ennis's words actually seemed true—that he was one healthy kidney away from a life-changing turnaround, one healthy kidney away from having the strength to hike down to a decent fishing hole, from being able to make good on a decade-old promise to fly to Los Angeles.

The garage door was frozen shut. Even if he could have gotten it open, his little truck didn't stand a chance out there. At least a foot of snow filled his driveway and was still coming down, blowing and spinning in the wind as if three or four storms had all flown in at the same time from different directions, colliding outside his garage door.

A tremor of fear surged through his body. What if he couldn't get there in time? What if he wound up dying in his recliner waiting for the snow to stop falling? Well, that was ridiculous. He would figure something out. For the time being, there were only two things that mattered. He wanted to call Jo, and he needed to sit down and rest. As quickly as he was able, he headed back to his chair and picked up the phone from the end table.

"How's life in the desert?" he asked.

"Dad, I'm running late for work." He could nearly see her through the phone. She would have looked just like her mother at the same age, scrambling to get out of house with her purse bouncing against her hip.

"I just wanted to say hi is all."

"Okay, hi." She paused and he could hear her breathing. "Listen, Dad, I'm sorry, it's just not a great time right now. Can I call you later?"

"Sure," he said. He wanted to tell her about the snow, but what was the point in worrying her when there was nothing she could do a million miles away in California?

"Love you, Dad. I'll talk to you later."

Benjamin set down the receiver. He thought about calling the hospital to tell them he wasn't coming in, but he didn't have the number with him, and he didn't want to get up again; in fact, he wasn't entirely sure he *could* get up again. As he leaned back and closed his eyes, he thought about Margie's face when her body was finally giving in to the cancer those last couple of days. It had been so peaceful. She had gone through all that pain, and then in the end it was as if she had somehow learned to separate her consciousness from her failing body. The doctor had increased her morphine, but he never believed that was why. It was a grace, the preacher said, the first of two graces. First, God saved her from suffering, and then gave her a new and glorified body. That word. Glorified. It had never made sense to him. But a couple of months later he was talking with his neighbor, Madeline, and she said that her little dog was her glory. Those exact words, "She's my glory, that one." It had made sense to him then. Glory was something worth celebrating.

Benjamin fell asleep, his eyelids fluttering with exhaustion while the wind rattled outside, heaving against the house.

When he woke, it seemed as if dusk had already fallen, it was so dark inside. But according to the hands on the clock it was only two o'clock in the afternoon. For a moment, he was aware only of a vague feeling of worry lodged in his gut, and then he remembered: *failing kidneys, dialysis, snow.* Now the question formed in his mind: could he wait until tomorrow? He remembered the doctor describing how in renal failure, the patient's blood turns toxic, attacking its host. He didn't know how long his body could survive without dialysis. Doctor Ennis had said days not weeks, but now that it really mattered, he realized how many different things that could mean.

He decided to call the hospital. The phone was resting on the nightstand right where he left it, but he still didn't have the number. Again, he rocked and hoisted his body out of the chair. While he walked, he remembered how Jo had talked to him about making friends with his neighbors.

"I know my neighbors," he'd said.

"You know their names. That's not the same thing."

When Jo was in elementary school, Benjamin accompanied Margie to all the school events. He made small talk with folks in town. It didn't seem so hard at the time. But as Jo grew up and became more and more independent, the size of his world shrank. He worked, hunted, and watched television; occasionally, he went to church. Then Jo graduated and moved away, and then Margie got sick and died. Now it seemed practically impossible to start up a conversation with a neighbor or acquaintance. At the store, Benjamin kept his head down. Though he always bought the same things, he wrote out a list, so that he had somewhere to focus his eyes.

Passing under the archway into the kitchen, Benjamin felt the pressure building in his swollen ankles. He flipped through the phone book and found the number, but when he tried turning on the phone, nothing happened. It was dead. It was just a plastic nothing, completely and utterly useless. If it weren't for the fact that it would eventually come back online, he would have flung it across the room. He had the cell phone, but he'd never even turned it on.

He had just started working on some dishes, his fingers testing the water as it fell from the tap, waiting for the freezing water to turn warm, when he heard something banging. It sounded like a tree branch falling on the house, but then it happened again. Had the hospital sent someone up here looking for him?

When he opened the door, snow drifted into the house at his feet. Snowflakes danced into the living room as if it might start snowing inside, too, now that the weather knew he was in here.

A woman stood in the doorway, covered from head to toe: orange hunting hat, fogged glasses, brown scarf wrapped over her chin, yellow parka, black snow pants. She spoke, but he couldn't make out the words with the wind howling away.

"May I come in?" She was practically shouting.

"Oh, yes." Benjamin stepped aside. "I'm surprised to see anyone today." He forced the door shut behind her.

The visitor unwound her scarf and wiped her glasses with the inside of her hat. A long braid of thick black hair hung down to the middle of her back, swishing back and forth over her parka, scraping more snow onto the floor. She was in her mid-thirties, like Jo. He wondered if she had a portable dialysis machine in her vehicle outside. At the dialysis center, they had encouraged him to get a machine, but the idea of doing it himself was overwhelming. He preferred driving to the hospital, and, until today, it hadn't been a problem.

"I'm Daniella, Madeline's daughter. Your neighbor. Mom asked me to come check on you."

A flush of embarrassment came over him. To think that this woman had been sent out into this incredible weather just to check on him. Benjamin was suddenly aware of his ballooning body, his shirt fanning out over him like the walls of a tent. He sidled backward.

"How is your mother doing?" he asked.

"Oh, she's fine. We're hunkered down. I brought food and water and my husband's generator."

That was when Benjamin realized that the power had gone out. How stupid could a person possibly be? The house was dark, the phone dead, the television empty and quiet. And, yes, he had noticed it when he first woke up: the house was cold. Of course, with this wind, power lines would have been wiped out.

"We would've called," said Daniella, "But we didn't have a number for your cell phone." Madeline knew that his health wasn't good—that was all he'd told her—but it was enough, apparently, to put her on alert.

"I have one here. I can't remember the number off hand, but I've got it written down." The cell phone was a Christmas gift from Jo, who only made one short visit for the holidays. He'd had the thing for almost two months, but he hadn't even taken it out of the box. Daniella must have been exasperated at his stupidity—the fact that he didn't have the slightest plan in place for dealing with this storm—and now she was drawn into the situation.

He shuffled back to his chair and sat down. The dizziness was coming back, and his mind seemed incapable of latching onto anything. It was a swirl of confusion.

"Mr. Canning, do you think you would be able to walk across the street? I'm worried about leaving you here."

She reminded him of his daughter. He wasn't sure why. Jo had short hair; she had long hair. Jo had soft features and big sparkling eyes; Daniella had a hard face with a crisp jawline and pinched creases running across her forehead. Maybe the connection between the two was as unremarkable as their age, the fact that they were both confident young women of a generation who never asked a man to take care of the things men had always taken care of.

"My daughter lives all the way out in California. San Bernadino, can you imagine?"

"Mr. Canning, I can't just leave you here to freeze to death." She furrowed her brow. She looked as if she were trying to figure what it would take to lift the old man out of the house: two strong men? Three? A forklift?

"I do have a fireplace," he said. "There's dry wood in the garage."

He started rocking, preparing to stand, but she put up her hand. "Let me do it. You look tired." Daniella started down the hallway, slipped into the garage, and returned with an armload of wood. While she worked, he considered telling her about his dialysis appointment. But again, he didn't see the point in dumping his problem on someone else, especially when there was nothing to be done.

When she introduced the dry wood to the flame, it burst to life, crackling and popping.

"Are you sure you're going to be okay?" she asked.

He'd never actually said he would, but yes, he supposed so. He had heat and food. Now that he thought about it, there were some bottles of seltzer in the pantry. "Right as rain," he said.

"You turn on that cell phone of yours. I'm going to write my phone number on this newspaper right here. I want you to call if you need anything."

"It's in that cabinet over there," he said.

She walked back to the doorway and wound the scarf around her neck. Clearly, she was anxious to get out of there, and Benjamin could imagine what she would say to her mother about the condition of his home.

After Daniella left, it was quiet. He almost always kept the television running, and now there was nothing but the crackling of the fire. Picking up the remote, he tried inspiring the television back to life, pushing the on button repeatedly, anticipating the click and surge of life.

When Jo graduated college, Benjamin and Margie had traveled all the way to Pennsylvania, ten hours in the car. He groused the whole weekend—about the drive, the hotel, the long, over-blown ceremony. Things had been difficult at work, and that was at least part of the problem. They were making cuts at the lumberyard, and he was worried he would be laid off.

After the graduation ceremony, they went to a diner. The restaurant was decorated with signed pictures from the college's sports heroes, a few unknown actors, and a national politician who had stopped for five minutes on a bus tour. The pictures were hung in cheap plastic frames and dangled off-kilter on the wall. Jo started describing the jobs she was applying for (all in the fashion industry, all of them in Los Angeles and New York) and discussing her plans for the future. Margie went right along with everything while Benjamin kept looking down at his plate. He couldn't believe he had raised a daughter with such an unrealistic view of the world.

"Dad?" she said. "You're being really quiet."

He looked up. "Don't you get it?" he said. "This is all a pipe dream, Jo. This isn't the real world we're talking about."

"What do you mean?" she asked.

Benjamin was looking at the posters of these local heroes who didn't mean anything outside of this nothing Pennsylvania town, and he felt obliged to point out the obvious: she didn't go to the right college. She wasn't even one of the better students at the wrong college.

"Dad," she said, "Why are you saying this?"

"Because you're nothing special, and the sooner you figure that out, the better off you'll be."

Jo ran out of the restaurant, and Benjamin was confronted with his wife's rock-hard silence. The only thing Margie had said was, "I will not speak to you again," and she maintained that stance for several days. He could no longer remember what had finally ended her silence, only that when things finally returned to normal, things weren't the same.

Right before he and Margie got in the car to head back to Tennessee, Jo looked hard at him and said, "Daddy, why? I don't understand why you're doing this to me."

"What am I doing?" he said, the words coming out harsh like everything else that weekend. Words with sharp, accusing ends.

Jo was holding back the tears, but pain was evident in her face. He didn't know what to say. Since she was fifteen, she had consistently said that she wanted to leave their small town and never come back. She had dated two boys during college, and neither was white. One was black and the other was Mexican or something else, Puerto Rican maybe. Her career path made no sense to him. Fashion. He'd never heard of anyone working in fashion. It was as if she was rejecting every part of her heritage, everything about their family, everything about him. As they pulled away, he could see Jo in the rearview mirror. She stood with a hunch, the way people stand when they think they might throw up.

The only thing Benjamin managed to accomplish between naps was make the discovery that his cell phone was dead. When he pushed the on-button, it sprang to life. Then, almost immediately, it died. The battery light blinked, and the screen went dark.

The next time he awoke, he heard sounds coming from the front door. Knocking. The handle working back and forth. The tongue clicking inside. It was Daniella back before he'd been able to do anything about the mess.

"You don't look so good," she said.

"Not feeling great today." He teetered over to the kitchen where he stood with his hands against the counter, his fingers feeling like little balloons, like foreign objects soldered to his hands. "I was just going to do some picking up."

She shook her head. "You sit down. I'll pick up."

Benjamin tapped his bloated fingers against the countertop.

"Your daughter called. She heard about the storm, and she's worried about you. She thinks you were supposed to have dialysis today."

Benjamin kept standing at the counter.

Daniella started hustling dishes, glasses, and soup cans to the kitchen.

"We should do the wash, too, but I don't suppose that's happening anytime soon."

She stood right outside the kitchen. It was still overcast outside, the snow still coming down, but enough light was bleeding into the house from the front windows that he could see her clearly. She looked younger than before, her warm skin pinked with life. Her glasses were gone, and her eyes looked big and bright, the whites like pure cream. She'd let her hair down, and it was riffled with strings of blond and auburn, flowing in long curving lines like the trails formed where a clear river runs over a rock or a piece of driftwood.

"You're going to have to sit down," she said, "before I pick you up myself and carry you over there."

"You'll throw your back out doing that."

"Then you'll have your chance to take care of me, and we'll be even."

Benjamin obeyed, heading back to his chair. It felt miserable to walk. The swelling in his ankles must have increased, and it felt as if his skin was stretched as far as it could go, as if his feet had been screwed on too tight.

Daniella worked on the dishes, washing them in cold water. She brought more wood to the hearth, layering pieces onto the fire, blowing in the coals until flames grew through the top of the stack. Even when it was blazing, she remained hunched in front of the fire, not speaking.

He let the silence carry on for a while and then spoke. "It's very kind of you to do this for me," he said.

She chewed on her lip, and he knew she was working on words.

"Who would have thought that today would have turned out like this?" he added.

"The day hasn't finished turning out, has it?"

"No, I guess not."

The fire was wild and hot, lighting up her face in flashes like a camera going off again and again, as if her picture were being taken by a flock of unseen photographers. With her back turned and the fire glowing, he saw a wound behind her ear, red and crusted over. The sore was strangely, perfectly round.

"I called my husband," she said. "Just before I came over here. He has a four-wheel drive and chains."

Benjamin shifted in his seat, shaking his chair.

"I wish you hadn't. We should wait this out."

"He'll be fine."

This very minute, then, a man was driving up the mountain in his truck. Flare sides, probably, chrome steps jutting out below the doors, the roaring engine pushing through the snow like an angry beast.

Daniella looked peaceful now, sitting by the fire, and now, instead of Jo, she made him think of Margie when she was young. He could never figure out what happened to their marriage. All he knew was that at some point he preferred leaving to coming home. And once he grew acquainted with the feeling, it grew. Like his swollen ankles and distended belly. Once something starts, it never seems to stop.

For a while, they sat there together in the fire's glow. She held her knees to her chest. He touched his fingernails, and flexed his hands, and nodded off a couple of times. Another hour passed before Daniella's phone rang. Her husband was unable to make it up the mountain. In some places, the snow was so high it swallowed his fender. Outside, dark settled on the mountain. She hung up.

"I'm sure they'll get it plowed out tomorrow," she said.

Daniella insisted on staying with him, and Benjamin insisted she take the couch, while he slept in the chair. Somewhere in the middle of the night, half-conscious, Benjamin heard a sound. At first, he thought it was a cat, though he hadn't had a pet in the house since Jo left home. As his mind became more alert, he realized it was Daniella crying into her pillow, trying to muffle the sobs.

Suddenly, it occurred to him why Daniella had come home to Madeline's without her husband.

"Is that why you came home? To get away from him?"

She turned to look at him. In the dark, her face was no more than a shadow. "People always think it's the same old story, but it isn't always."

He didn't say anything. In his experience, it was always the same old story between men and women.

She started crying now, her chest shaking like she had the hiccups. "Oh God," she said. "I'm sorry."

"It's all right with me," he said.

"I can't cry in front of my mother. I guess I've just been holding it in."

He wondered what kind of man could do that to someone he loved. Maybe it wasn't love at all, or maybe it was a different kind, a burning type of love that can't be soothed except in flame.

In a few minutes, her crying wound down. Daniella stoked the fire, and when she was done, she leaned back against the brick hearth, and the flames grew, and he could again see her.

"You shouldn't have called him," he said.

Talking face to face, the sore was hidden behind her ear. It seemed wrong that something so significant could so easily be made to disappear.

"He feels terrible," she said. "And he owes me."

Benjamin shook his head. He was hidden in the shadows, and he didn't know if she could even see him, but he shook his head anyway, unsure what to say, wanting to discredit the idea that this debt could ever be paid off.

The rest of the night his pain grew worse, his gut twisted into knots. His hands were so thick he could barely see his knuckles, and his fingers were going numb. He was feverish, drenching his blanket with sweat, slipping in and out of sleep.

In the morning, the sun rose, and they could see that the storm was past. Daniella turned her phone back on and called 9-1-1. She was running out of battery.

"They're waiting for the plows," she said, "but they'll come when they can." She walked to him and put a hand on his shoulder.

"I want you to tell me that you'll take care of yourself," he said. "Consider it the last wish of a dying man."

"You're not dying."

With every passing moment, the light was growing stronger. After the density of the storm, the brightness was staggering.

Suddenly, an idea occurred to him. "I can't live in this house any longer," he said. "I'm moving to Knoxville, and I want you to live here."

"You can't just give me your house."

Benjamin barely skipped a beat. "I know it's not in very good shape, but I'll get it fixed up. All it really needs is new carpet."

"And a new kitchen," Daniella added.

He was revived as he spoke, the pain and weakness of his body momentarily forgotten. "Once you get on your feet, you can pay rent. But not until then."

Daniella smiled. "We'll see," she said.

He rested his head against his chair. At this point, speaking was an exertion, breathing a labor. He knew his body was failing, but he also knew that the roads were being cleared and an ambulance would come before the end of the day. He might die, it was possible. Or he would die another day. If he was honest with himself, he'd given up hope of receiving a kidney, although death didn't seem as frightening as it had even a few hours ago.

It was so bright now, so cold and bright, that he could see every little detail of the world around him, every speck of dust in the air, every fiber in the carpet, every color and strand of Daniella's hair.

The momentary feeling of hope had now expired. The fire was dying, smoldering. In a moment, Daniella would take the poker and stir the ashes, uncover the coals, and heap on more dry wood. It was predictable. She was predictable. Just like him. He would die in this house. He would never travel to Los Angeles, where he knew he would be proven wrong about everything, where he would see for himself that everything Jo had said was true—that Darren was a good man—that she was happy—that the life she chose was better than the one she left behind.

Laura-Jean

I WAS FIFTEEN YEARS OLD when Laura-Jean arrived in our town. The year was 1942. Her father had received the call to our Methodist church, a big city preacher who fit our little New Hampshire town like the proverbial round peg to the square hole. Then there was Laura-Jean, who joined me in the freshman class. She had the goods. She was pretty, kind, and unflappable, and it wasn't long before she had climbed high above myself in the social strata of our school, while I remained locked into place. Middle of the road, Chet, now and forever.

Of course, I was infatuated with her. That year, I went to the movie theatre a half dozen times to watch the film, *Casablanca*, with Humphrey Bogart as Rick Blaine, pulling Ingrid Bergman into his gravitational field. I never asked my parents' permission, knowing it wouldn't be granted. Instead,

I would make an excuse and then walk down into town from our hilltop neighborhood, passing the row of strong-armed elms at the bottom of the hill, across Main Street, and into the film house, where I sometimes paid and was sometimes waved through by a friend running the projector.

While the movie ran, I watched Bogart as if I were trying to break a secret code. And then, later, when I was alone in my room, or during one of the lulls in the school day when there was nothing else to occupy my attention, I would imagine Laura-Jean and myself finding one another in Paris, the crunch of the war approaching from the eastern front, the two of us thrown into a desperate romance. In my dreams, Laura-Jean's primary attribute, apart from her luxurious hair and bright smile, was her infatuation with myself, and it was disorienting when I would then pass her in the halls, managing to elicit only the most commonplace of Laura-Jean smiles, the one that was handed out to every acquaintance, as if she were running for mayor of our little town.

My only connections with Laura-Jean were through church and Greek—a course of study that I took because I was interested, and that she took because her father insisted. Girls did not typically study the classics at that time, but Laura-Jean's father treated his only daughter like a son in regard to her education, another mark against his reputation.

⋅⋙⋅

At the beginning of the next school year, I walked into Greek class on the first day of the term, and she waved for me to come and sit in the open seat behind her. I don't know why she chose me that day. Her girlfriends weren't in the class, and neither was Charlie Fournier, a jock who often slipped over to the girls' table at lunch, squeezing in next to Laura-Jean on the already busy bench, his body in contact with hers even as they sat together. Still, it surprised me, and maybe she surprised herself. Maybe the idea popped into her head the way frogs leap suddenly into the water, or maybe all of those times when she greeted me in the hallways had been full of meaning after all—a recognition that we were alike in some important way. However it came about, from then on, just before class started each day, she would turn around in her seat, lock her leaf-green eyes onto mine and ask me a question.

"Chet, don't you think this war is just awful? Daddy says that men are dying in absolute heaps."

Or, "Do you ever wish you were old enough to join the fight?"

Or perhaps something much more mundane. "What on earth do you think I got on my dress? Chet, have you ever seen anything like it?"

I didn't know what she had gotten on her dress, and I had never wanted to go to war, being certain I would wind up in those piles of dead bodies. I had never been particularly cunning, and I suspected that I wasn't brave either. Still, when asked, I said yes, I had thought about going to war, because in all of those hours spent playing and replaying the *Casablanca of Chet and Laura-Jean*, I had many times turned myself into a war hero briefly on leave from the fighting or recovering from a wound in Paris. So I said, "Yes, sometimes I do."

One day, Laura-Jean turned around just as class was about to start and said, "Walk me home after school today." Our teacher was calling the class to order, and I just managed to nod my head in agreement before Laura-Jean shifted her attention back to the front of the room, leaving me to stare at the white skin showing above the collar of her shirt.

Our school was built on what had once been a farm on the edge of town, and the path leading to the village traveled through a hay field and then a short section of woods. I will never forget how it felt to walk the path into town that day with Laura-Jean. It was well into September by now, but a long, dry summer was hanging on. The air had a salty sweetness, the grasses languishing for want of rain, their cracked tops opening wide and perfuming the air. I too was ready to burst, not from the heat, of course, but from the incredible air of possibility.

The grass was high in the field. The bulbous tops of the timothy swayed in the afternoon breeze, bending and bending, and then, when the wind took a breath, gently returning to their place. At one point, a groundhog wandered into the path, froze, and then scrambled back into the weedy wall. We had been among the last to leave school that afternoon, and we were alone.

"Oh, it's so lovely," she said, as if the goodness of the world was simply too much to bear.

I don't know why I said what I said then. It is one of many instances in my life when I have regretted my words even as they were falling out of my mouth, unable to keep my finger from poking into the sorest spot, the place where the flesh is already bruised and swollen. "My mother complains about your father all the time," I said.

She looked at me in confusion and stopped walking. "That's a terrible thing to say."

"Well, I don't agree with her," I said.

Laura-Jean turned away from me. Her hair was brown, tinted with red like fallen pine-needles, and it caught the afternoon light in a way that made it look so rich and alive, I felt that if I reached out and took hold of a bunch, I could crack it open and find milky sap hiding inside.

I thought she might be crying. Easing toward her, I put a hand on her shoulder. "It's okay," I said.

When we started walking again, she took my hand. I remember wondering how firmly I should grip it. I didn't want to squeeze her too hard, but I didn't want to lose her either. As we passed through the woods, I noticed how the tallest pines swayed and circled while the shorter trees watched. When we came out to the street, she let go and then led me through town to her house, seated just around the corner from the church. Her parents were sitting on the porch, her father with a stack of books resting at his feet.

"Heigh-ho," he said. "Look what we have here."

"Dad," she said. "Don't embarrass him."

Laura-Jean walked up to the porch, and I remained standing on the sidewalk, looking up at the three of them until it was clear I wasn't going to be invited in.

For the rest of the week, I anticipated a recurrence of our after-school walk, Laura-Jean turning around before class and repeating her invitation. Every day, I was disappointed. Laura-Jean was the type to linger in the hallways, talking with friends and remembering a question she'd been storing up for one of her teachers. I kept thinking up excuses to remain after school throughout the week. I talked with teachers, checked the office for a missing sweater, and just generally hovered. She was nowhere to be found.

Finally, on Friday afternoon, I walked into Poppy's, the drug store, and found her sitting at the booth with her friends, Betty, June, and Charlie. A gaggle of kids flocked around the shop, juniors and seniors lining the counter with Cokes and Moxies. I approached her from behind, tapping her on the shoulder just like I would have in Greek class.

"Oh, Chet," she said, turning. She looked as if she had been caught doing something she wasn't supposed to, her smile crooked and forced.

"I haven't seen you much this week," I said.

"I've seen you in Greek," she said. "Same as always."

"They're out of Coke," inserted Betty. "No ice cream either." There were shortages of sugar and butter.

"The trials of the war effort," said Laura-Jean. "I suppose there's sherbet."

"I suppose there is," said Betty.

"Sherbet's fine with me," I said, though I would have preferred ice cream.

"Chet here wishes he could go to war," Laura-Jean said.

Immediately, a fire of embarrassment exploded inside me like it had been doused with gasoline and gone up with a roar, the heat of it lighting up my eyes and flushing my cheeks and forehead.

Charlie smirked. "That's great, Chet," he said. "Real heroic." The three of them laughed, Laura-Jean employing her bright smile, white teeth flashing, head tossed back, so that I could see into her nostrils. I turned to the side, looking at the counter, which was running away from me to the soda fountain. I pretended like I was trying to get Poppy's attention in an effort to place an order, but with each passing moment, it was becoming more and more clear that I wasn't going to be able to keep myself from crying.

"Well," I said, as casually as I could manage. "I should get going," and then I turned and walked away, hot tears burning my eyes and blurring my vision even as I made for the door.

At church that Sunday, I successfully avoided Laura-Jean. It was easy enough to accomplish, since she always had people around her, grasping for her attention. I did not escape her father, who stepped in front of me just as I was about to leave for home and recruited me to work at the parsonage that week after school. He was adding a garage to the building.

He didn't need my help. That was clear on the first day, when he spent most of his time showing me what to do. I didn't even know how to swing a hammer let alone frame a building. I spent nearly all my time watching Reverend Akins, who seemed consumed with his own energy, his spry legs bending in exaggerated gestures.

We worked for a while, and then he said we should take a break. I sat on the porch while he went inside. Just when Reverend Akins disappeared, Laura-Jean walked onto the porch, sitting down beside me. As soon as I saw her, I understood that our meeting had been arranged.

"Chet," she said.

I didn't answer.

"Chet, I feel terrible about what happened at Poppy's."

"Yeah?" I said.

She put a hand on the center of my back, and I let the feeling, the pressure her hand made, seep into me. It was like magic the way it worked on me, my muscles relaxing, my anger dissipating like light drowning in water.

"I don't know why I said that—there's no excuse, none at all."

I looked down at my hands and wondered what would happen if I reached over and touched her leg. Would she squirm uncomfortably, slap my hand away, or might she allow it to remain?

We talked for a minute, and then I straightened up, stretching my back, and I noticed her looking up at me. It was a strange look she gave me. It was like she was searching for something—like I was the keeper of a key, a key that she needed to get where she was going, and she was wondering where I'd put it.

"I should go help your dad," I said.

For a while, Laura-Jean and I were friends. We stopped one another in the hallway between classes, and we walked home together from school. Sometimes, she would appear next to me at my lunch table, leaning in, Charlie Fournier looking on from where he sat with the rest of the baseball team. We talked about the war and the news reports that came rolling in from Europe and the Pacific theaters. It was what we had— Greek and the war—and the shameful thing is that I was thankful for what we had, even though it meant other people losing their lives half way across the world. Nothing mattered as much as an opportunity to get closer to the girl I wanted. And what I wanted was to have her—in the Biblical sense. If I'm being honest, I was never all that interested in friendship.

It was about a month later—a month after the conversation on her parents' porch—when it happened, the party at Charlie Fournier's house. It was October now but not too cold yet, and with the crowd of people in the house, it was warm inside. I remember sweating and how my pants felt tacky against my legs. A couple of kids had snitched booze from their fathers, and a circle of boys were flipping shots of whiskey into their mouths and then practically choking as it went down, the rest of them guffawing at the faces the drinker made. I knew better. My mom would smell the whiskey on my breath. She kissed my cheek when I came into the house at night, and I knew why.

I had been at the party for a while, and I hadn't seen Laura-Jean or Charlie. It was strange she wouldn't be there, but Charlie even more so, though I didn't care to see him. After playing a few hands of cards, I decided to take a break from the house and its warm, tired air. I slipped out the back door to a long wooden porch.

The cool night tingled against my damp skin and puckered into goose bumps. For a few moments, I stood on the porch, but then, noticing the large harvest moon sitting low and fat in the sky, I wandered out into the yard to get a better look and stand in its wide spray of light.

There was noise coming from the house, the whooping sounds of teenagers leaking through the closed windows and doors. But then I noticed something else—there were sounds coming from the barn as well. Shuffling and scraping sounds and then a voice. It was Laura-Jean.

"Charlie, don't. Charlie, stop it. Charlie."

"Come on," he said. "Jesus."

I moved as quietly as possible toward the barn, my feet swishing in the grass and crunching uncomfortably on the weedy stone walkway. Outside the barn, I paused for a moment, understanding through intuition how important these next moments would prove to the course of my life. Seeing without seeing as Jesus liked to say.

I couldn't see inside. There were gaps in the barn boards, but not enough light to make anything out, except for the voices now turned to whispers. I thought I could slide the door an inch or two, but it was jammed, and when I strained harder, the door jerked into motion, the metal hardware letting out a groan like a shout in the night.

I found myself staring at the forms of two people, startled, and lit up in a gawking streak of moonlight. First was Charlie, naked from the waist down, his bare skin white as chalk. And then beneath him was Laura-Jean. I couldn't see much of her. I could see her bra and her stomach, her face and her eyes. God, those terrible, desperate eyes looking straight into mine.

For a long time, I told myself that I didn't know what was happening in that barn, that I couldn't have known for sure. But I knew—I knew from the moment I heard her voice when I was standing in the yard. I knew it when I saw the way his visible hand was holding her by the wrist. And what did I do? I peered into the barn, saw those helpless eyes, and turned away, coward that I was.

Again, I was embarrassed, only this time my embarrassment was more complicated. I looked at the stiff branches of an old oak tree, trembling in the wind, and felt the embarrassment of having witnessed something untoward, felt the embarrassment belonging to my gender for its many crimes, and more than anything else felt the embarrassment of knowing that I didn't have the guts to make it stop. I turned away and walked straight home, my legs lifting occasionally to a jog I was so desperate to get away from the thing that I had seen.

The next time Laura-Jean and I were alone together was the day of our high school graduation. I had avoided conversations with Laura-Jean since the night at Charlie's, but on graduation day my spirits were running high. The war had ended, and Americans were the new power in the world. I was bound for Dartmouth that fall, and a great life stretched out before me.

My parents celebrated my graduation by purchasing our family's first automobile. In the afternoon, when the ceremonies were over, I took the car out for a drive, cruising down to Main Street to show off. There was Laura-Jean.

"Hey there, Darling. Want to take a ride? She's a real fine jalopy."

Laura-Jean stepped into the car, pulled back her hair into a ponytail, and we were off, running into the countryside.

"Just like old times," I said.

She looked at me and shook her head. "No, Chet," she said. "It's not." Strands of loose hair were waving in front of her face and tickling her eyes. I kept driving until we were rattling over a rutted country road, the noise of the car unable to ward off the silence between us. I slowed the car and pulled over. I turned the key, and for a moment we sat there in the quiet of some nowhere hayfield.

"I'm sorry," I said. "I've been wanting to say that for a long time."

"Oh yeah, for what?" she said. She had retied her ponytail, but it didn't come out right, and she was doing it over.

"I don't know," I said, "For everything." I coughed into my sleeve and noticed that my heart was racing.

She leaned against the door of the car. "My God," she said. She didn't look at me when she said it but spoke the words into the door's leather lining. It was a prayer, a real prayer. I've learned to know the difference. She was pledging to the God of the Universe she was never going to forgive me.

"What?" I said.

"Chet," she said. "You're not a lick better than Charlie." I could see that she felt a jolt at saying the name out loud. It startled her, and it took her a moment to collect herself, open the door, and step out of the car, insisting on walking alone back into town before finally allowing me to drop her off at her house.

I've thought about the question a lot since then: "Am I better than Charlie?" I went to seminary and on to the ministry half for the sake of proving something to myself, though I've never gotten anywhere with that argument. When it comes down to it, I'm not a lick better than Charlie. She's right. But there came a point when I finally saw the past crystallizing into a knowable shape and saw that sixteen-year-old Chet was really a separate person from the one that I've become. When

I had that realization, not too long ago, I looked up Laura-Jean through an old acquaintance. I'd hoped we could go for another ride, try the conversation again, and see if it came out any different the second time around. But she had died. Turned out she had a bad heart.

Anyway, I don't think she ever needed to know the whole truth, the worst part—that while I felt guilty about my part in things, I was also jealous of Charlie, because he got to have her and I never did. That was the thing I never knew what to do with, and I still don't.

First Night

IT WAS THE MORNING OF New Year's Eve, and a dull light confessed the start of another winter day. In Vermont this time of year, the days were short. It was dark when Brian woke in the morning for work and dark when he drove home from the office. Even during the daylight hours, the world was grey and drab, an ever-present dusk.

The night before, Brian dreamt that the roof was covered with two feet of heavy snow. In his dream, he could feel the house sweating as it tried to hold the weight, could hear the rafters cracking under their burden—pop, pop, pop, like the last kernels of corn on the stove.

In reality, only a few inches had fallen, and much of that had blown away. Still, he started a pot of coffee—six cups, not the full pot he used to make—and went outside in sweats and a parka to shovel the roof. He pulled the garage door open and assembled the long metal claw of his roof rake, the coarse threading of the aluminum poles groaning as he twisted them together. He walked the circumference of his home, reaching toward the roof peak and dragging the shovel down to the eaves. Little cadres of snow fell to the ground, some of it landing on his boots. Soon his feet were aching with cold.

Inside, he poured a cup of coffee. He thought about carrying the wet socks downstairs like Amy would have, draping them over the utility sink to dry. Instead, he balled them up and threw them at the door to the basement. His phone was beeping. Text messages were popping up. They were from his friend, Charlie. It was porn.

"Classy."

He deleted the pictures. The kids were coming over tomorrow, and sometimes they played with his phone. And, of course, they would tell their mother. He could just imagine how Amy would react. "Courtney told me what she saw on your phone," she would say. She would criticize his behavior from every possible angle. It was an inappropriate use of his work phone. Did he forget that his children knew his passcode? Was he really okay with this sort of exploitation and objectification of women?

It was different for Charlie. Charlie was divorced, and his relationship with his ex was reduced to parent-teacher conferences and weekend hand-offs. "It's great," Charlie said.

"It's the best we've ever done. Even when we were dating, we fought, but now we're like BFF's."

Brian and Amy were separated but not divorced. They hadn't said much to the kids, except to reassure them that they were working on things. And they were. At least, they were going to weekly counseling, an ongoing reminder that they had a lot of history together, that they still cared about each other, and that they couldn't seem to stop fighting.

A couple nights before, after their last counseling session, he met Charlie at the bar. Before the separation, he didn't spend much time with Charlie outside work. But now, it was as if he was moved to a new group, a new team.

"How was it?" Charlie asked.

"Earth-shattering. Life-altering."

"That good, huh?"

They ordered drinks. Beer for Brian, martini for Charlie.

"Every little thing gets turned into some huge issue," he said.

Charlie put his index finger on the napkin under his glass and spun his drink around in a circle, a full three-sixty.

"Let me ask you something: when's the last time you got laid?"

"Two thousand six," said Brian. "Roughly." Ten years was an exaggeration but not ten months.

"This is the problem," Charlie said. "You've got all of this pressure built up inside, and it makes you very irritable. I'm sorry I have to tell you that, but I feel like I need to. As a friend."

Brian was staring at his drink, watching the bubbles rise to the top of the glass and thinking about something Amy had said during their session. It was after an argument died down, and she was looking at her shoes. She said, "If something doesn't change soon—I just don't know." She pulled back, but Brian knew exactly what she was threatening. After all, there was only one lever left to pull.

Charlie returned to his topic du jour: Brian's need for sex.

"At the core," he said, "we're animals with animal desires."

"She can't separate things," Brian said. "If there's anything wrong, then we don't have sex. And there's always something wrong."

"I'm not talking about Amy."

Charlie raised his eyebrows and took a sip from his glass. Brian followed suit. It wasn't as if this hadn't occurred to him. He had all the privacy in the world, and it was Amy who left him, taking the kids to a co-worker's rental property on the other side of town.

"Listen," Charlie said, "Ted's New Year's Eve party is coming up. We are going to go to that party, and we are going to get laid."

"Whatever happened to dinner and a movie?" Brian said.

He met Charlie at the mall for lunch. It was not his turf. For seventeen years, Amy had supplied Brian's wardrobe, combining suits, shirts, and ties for work, even composing casual outfits for weekends. Charlie was the only man Brian knew who dressed himself without any assistance, even when he was married. He wore tailored shirts and suits. He even tied a better knot than Brian. And women, Brian noticed, were always commenting. Commenting and touching.

They walked along the mall's main thoroughfare, falling into the flow of traffic. Everywhere Brian looked he saw couples. Old couples, middle-aged couples, young couples. How does a person end up like this—forty and single and hanging out in a mall with his only friend? Of course, he knew the answer. It was a reality he'd been having a hard time accepting. He had always succeeded in life: in sports, in school, in career. And when he married Amy, it was another victory. And then the kids came along. Now it was as if all of that had been undone.

"So what's the plan?" he asked.

"What do you mean?" Charlie was walking past storefronts, dismissing one after another.

"The plan for tonight. Meeting women."

"Oh, you know, looking good," Charlie said.

"Hence the clothes."

"Yes, the clothes. And then saying things—words—mostly in English."

"Charlie, I'm serious."

Charlie pointed across the hallway and headed for the *Banana Republic*. Standing at the entrance, he turned and looked at Brian. The two men stood eye-to-eye. They were the same height, each six feet tall, though they were otherwise entirely mismatched. Charlie was slender with a full head of dark hair. Brian, on the other hand, was thick, from his trunk-like legs to his broad chest, and all the way to his large round head, which was topped with thinning, blond hair.

"How did you meet Amy?" he asked.

"Physics," Brian said. "We were assigned a group project."

Charlie pursed his lips. "So you've basically never done this?"

"Basically."

Charlie pointed at a shirt—green with a thick gold thread punctuating the seams.

"This one," he said.

"I don't know," Brian said. He looked at the price tag. The shirt was sixty dollars.

Charlie took the shirt off the rack. "Sorry. You don't get to decide."

Brian walked to the register and paid.

They went to the food court for lunch. Brian hung the bag with the sixty-dollar shirt on his chair.

Charlie launched into his moo shu pork. "Here's the thing you need to realize: at a party like this, you're not going to be the only one looking to hook up. There are a lot of lonely women out there."

There was a din of noise in the food court. Speakers in the ceiling tweeted out pop music; kids shouted; workers at the restaurants banged and scraped as they harvested food from ovens, dug with metal spoons, refilled empty containers.

"You sound like a predator," Brian said.

"You know what I mean." Charlie was half listening while he tried to open a packet of duck sauce.

"Well," Brian said, "You've been a real help."

Charlie rolled his eyes. "Just wear the shirt, okay."

Brian went home, watched football, and drank a beer. He couldn't find his slippers, and his feet were cold. And he was tired. It was always this way when the kids weren't around. He wanted to sink into the couch and stay there. If it weren't for Charlie, he would have.

He texted Amy. He said he wanted to see the kids. Which was true.

"Sure," she said.

It wasn't that long ago when he would have been playful with her. He would have asked her what she was wearing, or told her that he needed help adjusting his lower back, or that he had something for her, and when she asked what, tell her it was a sausage. They used to laugh together.

He got dressed and brushed his teeth. He was going to splash cologne on his neck but decided, instead, to bring the bottle, along with a handful of necklaces his marketing firm designed for the city's First Night celebration.

Amy was in sweats. Her cheeks were pink with exertion, and though her hair was pulled back, flyaways danced over her head.

"What are you doing?" he asked.

"Cooking." This meant she was cooking multiple meals at the same time, stashing a week's worth of food into the fridge and freezer. In Amy's world, cooking was an event. Prepping a single meal was just *getting dinner ready*.

"You remember you have the kids tomorrow?" she said.

"I'll be hung over," he said, "but as long as they're quiet."

"Very funny."

The kids surfaced from the basement, heading for the kitchen, but stopped when they saw him at the door. They watched him, still unsure how to react to visits from their father. Courtney was twelve, and though she pretended she was fine, she would get fidgety when he saw her. It took hours for her body to settle down. Dirk, three years younger, seemed less affected, though Brian still worried about what all this was doing to him.

Reaching into his jacket pocket, he brought out three of his necklaces. He demonstrated how the magnetic clasp snapped together at the neck and lit the star. It was Brian's idea to incorporate his client's logo into a light-up necklace.

It was his biggest client, a large regional bank, and they were thrilled with the idea.

"We saw them," Courtney said. "We went downtown with Grandma, and they're everywhere." Dirk took one and started playing with the clasp. Brian hung one around his daughter's neck.

"Next time, gold would be nice."

"Don't hold your breath."

The kids headed for the kitchen, and he found himself once again alone in the foyer with Amy. He leaned back against the door. He was still wearing his jacket, and he felt a drop of sweat on the nape of his neck.

"What about me?" she said.

He held a necklace in his outstretched palm, and Amy picked it out of his hand. It was all wrong—the separation, visiting his own family on New Year's Eve. They should be together, watching a movie and waiting for the ball to drop.

Amy said, "This was a really great idea, the way it lights up."

He unzipped his jacket. Unfortunately, his problem had never been smarts. What Amy kept saying was that he was emotionally unavailable, an accusation he had a hard time arguing. But how was he supposed to be more available when he didn't spend time with her, when their only real conversations were in front of a therapist? And how could he feel close to her when she was so angry with him?

"New shirt?" she asked.

"What do you think? I'm not sure."

"I like it."

He knew she was wondering where he was going in his new shirt. Possibly she had already guessed it was Ted's party, which was somewhat infamous.

The kids headed back to the basement. Amy watched them, pivoting her shoulders and craning her long neck. How many times had he kissed that neck? Touched it with the tips of his fingers?

Again, she faced him.

"Tomorrow?"

"Yes, tomorrow."

Downtown, people were everywhere, appearing like ghosts from darkened streets and shadowed doorways, materializing under the effervescent gleam of frozen streetlights. The green stars—his green stars—rode the necks of practically everyone he saw, little green burning embers.

Brian stopped his car and waited for a group of college students to cross the street in front of him. The girls wore parkas and skin-tight leggings. He watched their long legs prancing across the street. His phone beeped. Another text message from Charlie. "Coming," he typed and pulled forward.

⋯⋯

Charlie stood in the middle of the living room with a woman who, in heels, was nearly as tall as he was. She wore a short skirt over tight leggings. Her top had a low back and openings for her shoulders.

"Here's Brian," Charlie said. "This is my friend, Leggy."

"Celine," she corrected. She pretended to punch Charlie on the arm. "Can I get you a drink?"

Brian nodded. "Looks like I've got some catching up to do."

She trotted away, touching the shoulder of an acquaintance with one hand and holding on to her skirt with the other. Amy would never even have considered a skirt like that.

Ted's loft was a true bachelor pad. A curved, oaken balcony swooped through a vaulted living room that must have been thirty feet high. On the first floor, there was a gas fireplace surrounded with built-in bookshelves. On the second floor, a full bar.

"A friend of Ted's," Charlie said, meaning that she was not a client or connected with a client, meaning she was fair game.

"This is pretty sweet," Brian said.

"Bachelorhood ain't so bad."

"Yeah, but who's got this kind of money?"

"Me – you," Charlie said, with a snorting laugh.

Celine returned with a pair of martinis and another woman. Her name was Donna—a red head, fresh-faced, one of the younger women in the room, somewhere in her early thirties, he figured. It wasn't ten minutes before Charlie and Donna left the conversation, heading for a darkened spot underneath the stairs.

Charlie said, "Hey, I've got something I want to show you," and they laughed and walked away. When Brian looked again, a few minutes later, the two were standing close, Charlie's hand resting on Donna's shoulder.

"Were we that boring?" Charlie asked.

"Tell me about yourself." Celine touched her bare shoulders. Brian thought she was trying too hard, but maybe he was overthinking things. Maybe it was just a straightforward situation that called for a straightforward response.

He talked about work. It was a better topic than his personal life. After a few minutes, Celine went for more drinks.

"And you're not married?" she said, when she came back. She pointed at his hand.

"Divorced," he said. "Two kids."

"Me, too," she said. "Divorced. No kids, though."

"No?"

"Kind of a long story and not very uplifting." She swept her dark hair behind her ears, and Brian watched her black eyelashes flicker, noticed the tender skin at the corners of her eyes. She was pretty, more so than he'd recognized at first. Of course, it could have been the martinis, but he didn't think so.

"I've got a secret," she said. She leaned toward him, and he could smell her perfume. "I'm kind of nervous. I haven't really done this. Not since. You know."

Brian smiled. "Me neither."

"One double date," she added, "but it was a disaster."

"Now that sounds like an uplifting story."

She adjusted her skirt, straightening the waist and tugging at the hem. "There's not too much to tell. He was a jerk."

"Not like me." Brian raised his glass.

"You do seem nice." She sidled closer and put her finger on the collar of his shirt. "I like this."

"I'm known for my fashion sense," he said. But she didn't laugh. Instead, she tilted her head slightly, a motion he recognized as an invitation. He reached out and put his hand on her hip. Now he did feel drunk, though he wasn't sure if it was the alcohol or the adrenaline pouring into his bloodstream.

"Maybe a beer this time?" she said.

Brian pulled away and climbed the stairs to the bar. He found two beers, held them by their necks, and looked over the railing. It was like Noah's Ark in reverse, pairs of humans exiting Ted's apartment two-by-two.

"Hey." It was Charlie. He took one of the beers from Brian, twisted off the cap, and took a sip.

"How about a daddy double date tomorrow?" he said. "I've got the kids."

"If I can convince the natives," Brian said. He saw Donna waiting by the bar. "Find your soul mate?"

"Something like that. What about you and Leggy?"

"I like her."

"Then what are you doing up here?" Charlie asked.

"I don't know." He walked away, heading back down the stairs toward Celine.

The last thing he would remember clearly from that evening was his conversation with Charlie on the balcony. There were other things that would come back to him as he recovered and his mind cleared. But these first revelations were fuzzy and indistinct: phrases, short-circuited thoughts, scenes that lurched through time. Celine taking his elbow as they walked to the car. White dashes on black asphalt. Spindly tree branches reaching out like angry arms. Dull green lights flashing like winter fireflies.

He was lying down. He shifted, trying to isolate the source of the pain, but it was everywhere: back, neck, arms, shoulders, abdomen. And his head ached, too, in such a way that made him wonder if it was possible to bruise the tissue in your brain.

Amy was there.

"You dumb ass," she said.

Brian thought about speaking, but the process of selecting words and pushing air through his throat felt overwhelming.

"Do you even understand what a dumb ass you are? Is it even possible?"

He tried shaking his head, but even a subtle movement in one direction caused his head to swim. His temples throbbed with every pulse in his veins.

"You—" she said and took his hand. Brian closed his eyes. Her hands were always cold. She had terrible circulation.

"Do you know what happened?" she asked.

"No," he whispered.

"You drove into a tree. You destroyed your car."

Sometimes, in his dreams, he would see something important, something he had been looking for, but then find that he was unable to reach out and take it. And that's how he felt right now, like there was something he should have been able to grasp but couldn't.

The next time he opened his eyes, Amy was gone. He saw the fluorescent lights overhead, caught the sharp aroma of bleach, and he knew he was in the hospital. It started coming back to him: Amy holding his hand, some of the events of the night before. He had a massive headache.

When Amy returned to the room, she was holding a large coffee in a paper cup.

"I'm sorry," he said.

She stood at the end of the bed, and even though she was only a few feet away, he couldn't focus on her. It was like trying to find the borders of a cloud. He was having a hard time with edges, with definition. It was difficult to see details, but he did notice one thing: her hair was flattened on one side of her head. Even with the fog in his brain, he was able to put the pieces together. Amy was cooking when he last saw her. She would have watched the ball drop with the kids and showered before bed. Sometime during the night, she was awakened by a call from the police. She threw on some clothes, drove to the hospital in the freezing dark. She would have been terrified, angry, and exhausted.

"Amy," he said. "I'm so sorry."

"You said that."

Amy tipped her head, and that's when he remembered Celine. They'd left the party together, holding hands as they walked the short distance to where he parked. He opened the door for her.

"Is she okay?" he asked.

Amy nodded.

After a few moments, his wife sat down in a chair at the foot of his bed. She placed her coffee on a tray table and started crying quietly.

"What is it?" he asked.

"I'm tired," she said. "And I was scared. You were unconscious, and they didn't tell me anything."

He reached out his hand, and she scooted her chair toward

him and took it. She stroked his hand from his wrist to the tip of his index finger. She let it go.

The more time passed the more he was able to understand. He had a concussion, and the doctors wanted him to stay another night. He was going to have to live without a driver's license, at least for a couple of weeks. He needed a lawyer. He would have to tell his boss. He would have to find Celine's number so he could call and apologize. Those were the basics—a growing list of tasks and consequences. But none of that compared to what could have happened. If his car had struck someone. If Celine had been injured. Or, conversely, if he had made it home with Celine and spent the night with her.

The next day, Amy drove him home. After what had seemed like weeks of clouds and intermittent snow, it was bright and sunny. The overwhelming light glared off the snow. He kept his eyes closed. He didn't have his sunglasses, and a headache was already coming on.

He followed Amy into the house, and it was when he was taking his shoes off that he remembered the kids. "Oh man, I was supposed to have the kids."

"You were," she said.

"I'm sorry."

"That's what you've been saying."

It was late morning, the second day of January. More snow

had fallen, and it was melting in the bright sunshine. Icicles hung from the roof like stalactites.

Amy insisted on staying. "You're under surveillance. Doctor's orders."

He sat down and rubbed his temples.

She sat down next to him. "I should be pissed at you," she said. "I am pissed at you. But I should be more pissed."

"Maybe it just hasn't hit you yet."

She fished in her purse and came out with a hair tie. She drew her long brown hair into a ponytail. "When I got that phone call from the police, for a moment, I thought you were gone."

Brian rubbed his eyes with the palms of his hands, and a memory returned from the night before. Three people were crossing the street. They were wearing the pendants. He saw them—those silly green lights—and swerved off the road. He remembered pulling the steering wheel hard to the side and then waking up in the driver's seat, his body stiff and cold, hearing Celine groan, watching big snowflakes land on the broken windshield. It was the fact that he saw and recognized the pendants, even in his drunken state, which saved him from leveling three people with his car.

Amy went to take a nap, and he watched his wife walk down the hall to her old bedroom and her old bed. It was rife with meaning: the car crash, Amy's presence in the house, the sun and the snow. It meant something; he just didn't know what.

He lay on the couch but couldn't sleep. Water drops landing on a hollow drainpipe barked like a cowbell. He found a pair of sunglasses and his boots and went outside. He moved the drainpipe, and then he picked up a tree branch and started knocking icicles from the eaves. There was something profound about the icicles, so hard and yet so easily broken, their sharp points rendered useless as they disappeared into the snow.

He felt dizzy, and he sat down on the concrete steps. The headache, which had been on the wane, was now surging.

Amy opened the door and looked outside, blinking.

"What are you doing? Come inside," she said.

He wanted to move, but it took him a moment to stand, open the door, and collapse back into the couch. Once he was settled, he leaned back, his sunglasses still on his face.

He could smell coffee brewing. Amy was moving around the house, doing dishes, and picking up. He heard her go downstairs and understood she had taken care of the wet socks he'd left on the floor. Finally, she poured two cups of coffee and sat down next to him.

He considered saying something about Celine. At some point, he would have to tell the story, and, of course, Amy would be angry. And who could blame her?

"Charlie called," she said. "He said you were supposed to have a double daddy date."

"Guess I screwed that up, too."

She was staring at him.

"What?" he asked.

"You look funny like that." She went back to the kitchen. She was wearing an old bathrobe, one that she used to wear years ago when their kids were little and the house was littered with toys and smelled like diapers.

"Hey Ame," he called. "What are you doing?"

"Just getting some lunch."

He could hear her working, sliding drawers and opening cabinets, her hands finding the things she was looking for in her old haunt. His wife was so near and, at the same time, so far away. The distance that separated them was like a canyon, dug deeper and deeper by a river of disappointment. She was lonely. He felt abandoned. They were both angry. The distance didn't seem that great, but whenever one of them tried to cross, they found that the river was a torrent.

He must have drifted off to sleep, because when he opened his eyes, Amy was standing in the doorway to the kitchen. She was looking at him again, like he was some sort of unexplained phenomenon, a stranger on the couch in his sunglasses. Like she had no idea what he would do next.

Barred Owl

When I met Darren, he already knew my name.

"Erika Bing," he said. "I know you. You're Vermont famous."

He wasn't the first person to call me Vermont famous. The first was my girlfriend, Shelby, who'd compared me with The Logger, a kitschy comedian, who showed off his sleeveless flannel shirts in local television commercials and emceed events. His shtick hadn't changed in a decade.

"Vermont Living?" I asked. My restaurant, Barred Owl, was featured in the prior month's issue. The article was terribly cheesy. It opened with the line, "Many have observed that the call of the barred owl sounds like the question, 'who-cooks-for-you?' Now we know the answer—it's Erika Bing." There were several photos in the spread, large and glossy: me with one of my signature dishes, lentil crusted chicken strips; me with my two managers at the front of the house;

me in my starched apron, displaying my knife for the camera, palms out.

"I actually *heard* you first," Darren said, referring to my appearance on public radio. "And then, I guess I saw something online."

"That's pretty creeper," I said.

It was Green Up Day, the first Saturday in April, and Darren and I were part of the same team of volunteers. The two of us had joined forces to remove a muddy truck tire from the riverbank. It must have been there for several years, because a small tree was growing through its middle.

I had closed Barred Owl for lunch and harangued my staff into volunteering. They were spread out, picking up soaked newspapers, plastic car parts, and bicycle tires—any and all of the things people toss into a river. It was a cynical move on my part. At our Thursday staff meeting, I talked about how our restaurant needed to establish roots in the community. I laid it on thick. It felt like my comeuppance when we were assigned this site, a stretch of woodland at a bend in the Winooski River that collected the river's detritus as the spring floods receded. The only member of my staff who had chosen not to participate was Shelby, who seemed to have a radar for shit like this. It smelled like a dump, like decomposition.

"Buckthorn," Darren said, referring to the tree inside the tire. "Invasive. It's a junk tree."

"Great analysis," I said. "Do you have a saw?"

We ended up lifting the tire above our heads and throwing it over the top of the spindly branches. After throwing the tire, Darren bent over.

"You okay?" I asked.

"Yeah, I think I pulled a muscle." He grimaced.

I started rolling the tire toward the parking area, where the trash was being picked up. Darren followed. He made a joke about letting me do the work. He said he was fostering equality. He was skinny and tall, with dark hair parted on the side. He wore square-rimmed glasses, and I could see a large tattoo at the base of his neck, sneaking out from under his shirt.

"Let me guess," I said. "Dealer dot com." Dealer was the epicenter of the local tech scene. A healthy portion of the young professionals in the area worked at their South Burlington campus, designing and managing websites for more than half of the nation's car dealers.

"Good try," he said.

We were walking uphill. I stopped for a moment to catch my breath. "Med student?"

"Nope."

"Ski bum?"

He smiled. His hand was on his abdomen, rubbing at a spot right below his ribs. Despite the fact that he was skinny,

I noticed that he had a bit of a belly. It was weird, but then again, bodies were strange. Like people, they didn't always make sense.

"Shit, that's all I got."

"Actually, I'm a pastor," he said.

"Oh... cool." I started rolling the tire again and tried to remember if I had said anything about Shelby—I didn't think so. "What kind? I grew up going to church."

He described himself as post-evangelical. "There are some things I still love about the evangelical church," he said. "But I'm in a different place."

"I thought you were going to say Lutheran or something."

"You're a bad guesser," he said.

When our work was done, Darren told me about this banquet for the homeless his church wanted to sponsor.

"At this point, it's just an idea," he said, "but the concept is to turn the soup kitchen on its head. Make it elegant. We'll provide clothes so our guests can dress-up. It will be a real celebration."

"Wow, that's so cool."

He gave me his card.

That night, after closing, Shelby and I walked back to my place. Most of the houses in the neighborhood were dark; almost everyone was asleep. On our walk, we passed a college house that was like an island in the sea of night. Every light was on; music seeped through the windows and doors. Despite the cold, a few kids stood on the porch, vaping.

"To be young," Shelby said.

"You are young."

"Not like that."

As we got ready for bed, I told Shelby about Darren and the banquet.

She turned away as she slipped off her black work pants.

"What?" I asked.

"You know what he's doing," she said.

"He didn't even invite me to church." I picked up my toothbrush. I held it in front of me while we talked.

"I promise you," Shelby said. "This will not end well."

Two weeks later, I did attend Darren's church. It had been a late night at Barred Owl, but I cajoled myself out of bed, leaving Shelby in a twist of sheets. She slept like the dead. At her apartment, she relied on a series of alarms to rouse her for morning meetings and still overslept sometimes. It took me a while to realize that I could grind coffee or walk around the house in my heels, click-clacking on the hardwood and it wouldn't wake her. Still, I snuck around as I got dressed. On the way out the door, I left her a note: "Out for the morning."

The city of Burlington was built on a hillside, on the edge

of a deep, glacier-dug lake. It was always windy. In spring, the breeze was bitter. It cut through my three-quarter length blouse, hurrying me to the entrance.

Lakeview was a new church, just a couple years old. It met in a remodeled warehouse with wide pine floors, wood beams, and heavy iron plates. It smelled like coffee and lemon Pledge. The space was divided into a lobby and a sanctuary. The sanctuary had seating for about a hundred, and it was about sixty to seventy percent full. Almost everyone wore jeans and sipped on a cup of coffee from a self-service station in the lobby.

When we were searching for a building to house Barred Owl, we looked at a warehouse like this one. Our team loved the industrial feel, but there were zoning issues that required a waiver. While we were making inroads with the city, a restaurant went up for sale on the waterfront. We jumped on it. The building was perfect. It needed only minor renovations, and as a bonus, it was close enough to my house that I could walk from my south end neighborhood.

Coffee in hand, I took a seat in the back. I was just getting settled when a middle-aged woman stood up in front of the congregation to offer a welcome. "There's lots of coffee," she said. "Please don't make me throw it away." She went over the order of the service in lieu of a printed bulletin. "It's a waste of paper," she said. "What we're doing is really simple. A time of singing, a message about Jesus. That's pretty much it."

The music was super chill. One guy played guitar and harmonica. Another banged on a cajon. A young woman played mandolin. I loved it. A couple of the songs were old hymns and a couple were new to me. I sang along as I figured out the music.

When the singing was over, Darren stepped to the front. As promised, he talked about Jesus. He used a music stand instead of a pulpit and never seemed to look at his notes. He wore a long-sleeve shirt that covered his tattoos. The message was about the passage where Jesus said, "Judge not lest you be judged." Darren really went deep with his message. He talked about why we feel the need to judge others—about the difference between evaluating whether others are safe or trustworthy and offering condemnation. The first, he said, was discernment. The second: judgment.

While he was speaking, I got this feeling that I sometimes get in church. It had been a long time—years and years—since I'd experienced it. It's hard to describe, but the best way I can think of is to say that I was feeling both highly alert and completely relaxed. I looked around at people, and I could feel that we were connected in some very profound way, even though I didn't know anyone. The Apostle Paul talked about the peace that passes all understanding, and that's another good way of describing it. Peace plus transcendence.

When the service was over, I greeted a couple of people

who were sitting nearby and then escaped to the lobby. I was just making for the exit when Darren caught up to me.

"Erika Bing," he said. A smile bloomed on his face. "Welcome to Lakeview."

I pointed out that there was not, in fact, a view of the lake. "Basically, the entire thing is a lie."

"The view is metaphorical," he said.

"Oh, okay."

"So… what did you think?" he asked. Darren looked tired, his skin pasty. Preaching must have taken a lot out of him.

I leaned toward him. "I fucking loved it," I whispered.

"Great," he said. "Awesome."

Burlington, Vermont was like a teenager. It mocked the idea of coolness while simultaneously obsessing over it. There was always a hip new spot, a designation that seemed to last for a couple of months, max. At the moment, Barred Owl was the place. People liked the sense of playfulness, I think, the pretension and lack of pretension all in one package. Steak tartare was on the menu, and so was chicken strips.

I was intentionally messing with my guests' expectations. It was part of the appeal. But the food was what kept people coming back. My mantra was all-out flavor. Don't worry about stereotypes—the only question was whether it tasted good. We did churros as an appetizer, salmon in a bowl of herbed crème fraiche, aged steak, buckwheat pancakes with truffled eggs, the aforementioned fried chicken strips with three, rotating dipping sauces. Some of our meals were typical of fine dining. Others you could order at Denny's.

It was a good thing people liked the restaurant. As my accountant, Rick, often said, I was a better chef than business owner. Our expenses were high and our prices low. Now we were riding a wave, and even though we were making money (a rarity for a new restaurant), we were barely making a dent in our mountain of debt. Rick wanted me to raise our prices, increase everything by twenty percent, which seemed outlandish.

I had given plenty of tours, showing friends, investors, and journalists around the back of the house, down to the cellar, and then to the bar for a drink. Darren was the first person to whom I served food on a Monday, opening Barred Owl for a single table. I don't really know why I did it. We had just met. But I liked Darren. He was cool, and I wanted to impress him. I also grew up in a culture where the pastor was shown special deference.

"I heard the chicken strips are amazing," Darren said as we sat down. At church, he'd had this bright look in his eyes, but now it was gone. They looked sunken and shadowed.

"We don't exactly have a full menu." No one had started the fryer, so we couldn't do chicken strips or churros. We were also out of crème fraiche, so no salmon.

"I love pancakes," he said.

"Good. That's all we have." I snuck back to the kitchen where one of my chefs was working on inventory and asked for two plates of pancakes. We served our pancakes with a flight of maple syrups from a farm on the Canadian border. I put together the flight, poured two cups of coffee, and circled back to the table.

"I've been meaning to ask you about the name," he said.

I got this question a lot. "I think owls are amazing," I said. I tapped my finger on the table. "Also, there's this thing about barred owls. When they mate, they have this ritual of calls, noises, and movements called a duet. It's how they pair—how they find each other. Which is how we make food, right? We make pairs."

"It's a great name," he said. "Great logo."

I ran back to the kitchen and grabbed our plates of pancakes and eggs. I set them in front of us and watched Darren take his first couple of bites.

"The food is… ridiculous," he said.

I let out a breath I didn't know I was holding in.

We kept talking until Darren interrupted and pointed at my plate.

"You haven't eaten a thing," he said.

"I guess I'm distracted. It was a busy weekend."

"I bet," he said.

I had a bite of food prepared, held in the tines of my fork and ready to go into my mouth. "I've got a joke to tell you,"

I said. "A lesbian walks into a church called Lakeview that doesn't offer a view of a lake."

Shelby heard about my lunch with Darren, and we started arguing about it at work. Even though it was a weeknight, we were slammed, and our conversation took place in fits and starts as we passed each other, always in the middle of a task.

"You're like a moth to the flame," she said. She was pouring a glass of wine and filling a another with soda at the same time. "Moth. Flame."

"That's so unfair." The kitchen staff was in the weeds, and I went back there to help. For half an hour, I plated dishes. Then I returned to the bar. Shelby was mixing a drink, and I sidled up next to her. "You're jealous," I said.

She shook her cocktail shaker with more force than was necessary. "Am I?"

Stewing, I went to check in with my hosts. I wanted to leave, to have some room to breathe, but there was no way. I looked around the restaurant, and every table was seated. The bar was two rows deep.

I closed my eyes. Over the din of the restaurant. I heard Rick, the accountant's voice: *This problem isn't going to solve itself.*

Later, when things finally died down, I cornered Shelby. I saw her go into the cooler for a keg and followed her. It was freezing. I could see her nipples through her shirt. She got cold easily, and when she did, her nipples turned hard as stone. I joked that she could cut glass with those things. If we were ever in a car accident and couldn't get out of the vehicle, she could carve a hole in the windshield and lead me to safety.

"We need to raise the menu prices," I said. "Across the board. That includes alcohol." I asked her to let me figure out the church thing. I promised I'd be careful.

"Okay," she said. She blew her hair out of her face.

Later that week, I was home, making drinks at my kitchen island. Shelby was over. She had her computer open, and she was feeding me directions for negronis. I was describing my conversation with Darren.

"It was weird," I said. "He was very non-committal."

"Like he was hiding something?"

I poured the gin, swirled, added the Campari, swirled. "No," I said. "I don't know."

Shelby couldn't understand my attraction to church. I grew up in a suburb of Cincinnati, and my family attended a large, very contemporary-feeling Baptist church, a church that "stood in opposition to alternative lifestyles." If you were gay, you couldn't be baptized or hold leadership roles unless you committed to a life of celibacy. It was deeply hypocritical. Anyone could commit any sin and be forgiven. Unless you were queer. But it was also my community. Growing up, my family's whole circle of friends were from church. I was baptized there. We used the gym for anniversary parties and wedding receptions, even my flute recitals. Most of my close friends were from my church, and our youth pastor was this cool guy, who knew about music, and art, and talked to us like we were adults when no one else did. When I stopped going to church, it left a massive hole in my life. I had tried explaining all of this to Shelby. She thought there was an easy answer—just attend an open and affirming church, UCC or Episcopal or Lutheran. I'd tried. But I hated the music—church choirs of warbly old ladies, organs wailing. They were populated with aging civil rights crusaders, a handful of young families, and always the token gays, usually the type that had grown up in the liberal church and never left. It wasn't my scene. I'd gone to a few open and affirming churches, one for a couple of months. But in the end, the experience made me even more angry, knowing that I couldn't go back to my own church.

I believed that I could be gay and still be the type of Christian who accepted the Bible as God's Word. The relevant passages in the Old Testament didn't matter; Jesus nullified the Jewish purity law with his teaching. In the New Testament, there were only three passages that condemned gay lifestyles. Three. And these texts were written during a time when gay relationships were between men and boys. There was no concept of a healthy, committed relationship between people of the same sex. For his part, Jesus didn't say anything about the topic. Nothing. Zip. Nada.

Shelby reminded me to add the vermouth.

"Yeah," I said. "I know."

"This church," Shelby said. "It may be a gentler version of what you grew up with, but it's the same deal."

"Yeah," I said, "I know."

On our first date, Shelby and I went to this cidery up in the mountains, an hour from Burlington. There was a bluegrass band playing. I don't normally listen to bluegrass, but it was perfect for the setting. The band soundtracked the evening like we were living in a movie. The banjo and the mandolin lit up the hollow; the slap and hum of the upright bass echoed off the hillsides.

For a while, we sat and listened to the music. Halfway through the set, we headed back to the tasting room for another cider and never made it back to the show. We talked and drank, and then we went for a walk down a dirt road, using the thin lights from our phones when the trees formed a canopy over the road, blocking the moonlight. While we were walking, we heard a barred owl. It was near but invisible, its voice rich and musical. At that point, the restaurant wasn't open yet, and I was still searching for a name. Shelby was the one who told me about the duet.

We went out several more times after that. To me, it was a

thing; it was clearly a thing. We never actually said that we were exclusive, but when I saw her with someone else, I was shocked.

I was meeting my investors at a new farm-to-table restaurant that was the hot spot before Barred Owl. Right when we entered, I saw Shelby with another woman.

The worst part was that I started crying. I couldn't hold it back. Tears filled my eyes and brimmed over. One of the women on my team noticed.

"Are you okay?" she asked.

"I'm fine," I said. I forced a smile. "I must have gotten something in my eye." For the rest of the night, I did everything I could to avoid looking at Shelby and her date. When our table was seated, I rushed to get a chair facing in the opposite direction. When I walked to the bathroom, I tried keeping my eyes straight ahead. But I couldn't help it. I looked. It was just a glance, but I saw them, leaning toward one another. The tears came again. I stayed in the bathroom for way too long.

Shelby called me that night to try to straighten things out. She said it was an on-again off-again thing, and she wanted to end it in person. I wasn't sure if I believed her. I'm still not sure.

A couple of weeks after my first visit to Lakeview, I walked home on a Saturday night, alone in the dark. Shelby and I were taking some space. I needed space.

There was too much quiet in the cool of the evening. I

was actually relieved when I reached the college house and there were signs of life. I stopped in front of the house and peered inside. I could see blurred faces through fogged glass. A guy with a beard, who must have been sitting in front of the window; a young woman with long black hair, who kept reappearing; a skinny guy, tall with dark hair, who passed quickly through the frame, there and gone.

The next morning, I went back to Lakeview. Again, I sat in the back of the sanctuary, only this time, I kept getting out of my seat—for a coffee refill, to go to the bathroom, for coffee again. While Darren preached, I thought about what he had said during our conversation about sexuality: "Our church holds a diversity of views." You know someone's bullshitting when their words sound like they were written by a committee. He had floundered, spewing nonsense, until I made the mistake of letting him off the hook.

"I just want a place where I can belong," I'd said.

"Totally," he said. "That makes sense."

When the service was over, I lingered in the lobby. I needed to talk with Darren about the banquet for the homeless. I was going to tell him that I couldn't do it, not for a while, not with my restaurant still coming out of the starting gate. It was too crazy.

I was leaning against one of the large wooden posts when a woman approached me. Her name was Lisa, a nurse at the

University of Vermont Medical Center. She had curly dark hair, the kind that looked like coiled springs. Even though she was friendly and cute, I couldn't focus on the conversation. I was looking out for Darren and fighting back tears. I didn't know where it was coming from, this wave of emotion, but I wasn't going to be able to hold it back forever.

By the time I left, I was practically running. The tears were starting. I was like a woman without an umbrella, trying to beat the downpour. I opened the door and fiddled with my keys. I started the car and shifted into drive. Then I saw Darren. He was waving at me, walking toward the passenger side.

"I'm glad I caught you," he said, climbing into my car.

I took a deep breath and wiped the tears from my cheeks. He didn't seem to notice.

"Listen," he said. "I wanted to apologize about our lunch. Sometimes, I get kind of wiped out. I'm not trying to make excuses. I'm just saying that I wasn't at my best."

"Okay," I said. I was holding the bottom of the steering wheel with my fingers.

"Of course, you're welcome at Lakeview," he said. "I'm supportive of you. And I want you to know that."

The tears started again. I motioned toward the glove box. Darren opened it, found a napkin, and handed it to me. His hand was cold.

"Are you okay?" he asked.

I nodded, shrugged.

"When we were talking at your restaurant, what I was trying to explain was that it isn't just about me. Churches are made up of people, and I can't guarantee that every person will accept you." He touched his forehead. "Most people will; this is Vermont, after all."

"It is," I said. It made me want to laugh, the idea that Vermont was this special place for gay people, where all our problems disappeared.

"Hey, listen, I really need to go," he said. "You sure you're okay?"

I nodded.

When Darren got out of my car, I saw him rubbing at that same spot, just below his ribs. It had been over a month since Green Up Day. It seemed strange that it would still be sore, and for the first time, I wondered if there was something wrong with him. He was pale and distracted. And he looked frail. He looked like he never slept.

Adjusting the rearview, I checked my reflection. My eyes were bloodshot, and I looked old. I was only in my mid-thirties, but I already had crows-feet and these ridiculous lines across my neck. Even worse, wiry grays were ruining my best feature: my hair. The grays were an abomination. I wanted to dye them out, but I didn't want to ruin my natural color—auburn with gold highlights—that people had always fawned over.

Later, I emailed Darren to tell him I couldn't do the banquet. I don't know if the event ever took place.

That Friday night, the host came back to the kitchen to tell me that a guest wanted to say hi. It was Lisa from church—the nurse.

"I'm sure you're busy, but I wanted to tell you how much I love this place," Lisa said. She was with a woman she introduced as a friend. Shelby always said I had the worst gaydar of anyone she knew. Again, I was proving her right. I had no idea.

"It's all my amazing staff," I said. While I talked with Lisa, I could feel Shelby's eyes on me. I knew she was behind the bar, pouring a drink, watching. When I'd told her I needed some space, she had been cool about it. But as the days turned into weeks, she was getting angry. Our conversations at work were getting terse.

As soon as I could get away from the conversation with Lisa, I headed for my office. Shelby, it turned out, was right behind me.

"Is this your way of breaking up with me?" she asked, closing the office door behind her.

She was five years younger than me, and I could see it in her skin. Even after a long shift—her makeup smeared, face pinked with exertion—her skin was smooth and supple. I probably looked like an ogre.

I insisted that I didn't want to break up. I made excuses. I said that I needed to work on some things. It was so hard to explain why I felt this need to withdraw. Back in high school, when my parents found out I was gay, they were upset at first, but then they transitioned into a long period of denial. We all just pretended that it was a phase. And it was exactly what I needed—time to figure things out for myself. With Shelby, there was a flash of intensity when we met, and it never stopped. I just wanted a moment to catch my breath.

"Isn't that what you do *with* your partner?" Shelby asked. Her button-down shirt was off-kilter, tucked into her pants an inch too far to the right.

"Maybe." I was feeling antsy about the bar with Shelby away from her post.

"It's fine," she said. "We had a bit of a lull." She could always read me.

I wanted to walk over and fix her shirt, untuck and tuck it again, smooth the wrinkles with my palms.

"Well," she said, "I need to get back."

Walking home that night, there was a commotion at the college house. As always, there was a party. Only on that night, despite the cold, it had spilled out into the yard. There was a huddle of people, and I could hear the concern in the voices of the onlookers. I wasn't going to intervene; I just wanted to make sure that someone called 9-1-1, if necessary. But when I got closer, I could see that it was Darren. Darren, my pastor, lying on his side in the grass. I'll never forget the way his arms were up over his head, his body bent at the waist. No one was doing anything. They were just watching, like a bunch of fools.

I was the one who called 9-1-1, who knelt down in the grass and held his hand. I was the one who greeted the paramedics when they arrived on the scene, who stepped back out of the way at their insistence. I was the one who watched, as they carried him away on a gurney and loaded him into the ambulance—who stared into the night while it drove away, lights flashing, sirens blaring, until it was gone.

It took me several steps to get in touch with Darren. He wasn't answering his cell phone, so I went to the restaurant and found Lisa's number in the reservation system. She said she didn't know anything, and she couldn't tell me anything either. But the next day, she called me back and gave me his room number at the hospital.

Darren didn't look like himself. He wasn't wearing his glasses, and his hair was combed wrong, pulled straight back instead of parted on the side. He was sharing his room with an old man, and the curtain was drawn between them. He was sitting up.

"There are some things I haven't told you," he said.

"You think?"

"I deserve that." He reached for his glasses. "Really, I haven't told anyone." He explained that he was diagnosed with Non-Hodgkins lymphoma almost a year ago. Then came surgery, followed by chemo. He took a leave of absence to hide his hair loss and recover. During his leave, he started taking pain killers and then came addiction.

"And going to college parties," I said.

"They had good stuff."

"Why didn't you tell anyone?" In the hospital gown, I could see how thin he was. His arms were spindles. His torso was like a boy's. I had known that he was thin, but now I could see that he was emaciated, except for that swollen stomach.

"My parents know about the cancer." A look came over his face. It was the look that he got when he was preaching and he presented a new idea, like it had just flown into his ear that very moment. "I guess I don't want people to treat me like someone who's sick. I told people I had surgery, but I lied about what it was for." He hadn't had chemo, so he kept his hair. But the trauma to his liver caused his gut to swell. "This guy," he called it, rubbing his belly.

I was thinking about my hair, wondering what it would be like to have chemo and lose all of it. I'd heard that when it grows back, it comes back as a completely different head of hair. Curlier. Finer. Darker. Lighter. "What's your prognosis?"

He adjusted his glasses. He said that his prognosis was good. They caught it early. The doctors think they got it before it spread.

I saw Darren one more time, at his home, before he left for rehab. I brought him a plate of chicken strips from Barred Owl. I was worried that the food was getting soggy in the take-away box.

"This is great," Darren said. "This is so kind."

I stepped into the house and looked around. There were books on the coffee table, a railroad clock high on the wall, a brick fireplace with a large rough beam for a mantel. I told him I wanted to talk.

Darren set the box of chicken fingers on the coffee table. He was still skinny, of course, but he looked healthier. His skin might have had more color—or maybe I was just imagining the change.

"I've never understood why churches were so hostile to the LGBTQ community," I said. "We aren't hurting anyone."

Darren shrugged. "Sex is a bogey man for a lot of people. People are infatuated with sex, and they're terrified of it."

I nodded.

Darren started eating one of his chicken strips. "Now that I'm clean," he said, "I'm famished. I eat nonstop."

He sat down and I took a seat across from him. I fidgeted. I was feeling upset again. Tears huddled behind my eyes.

"But what about you? What about your church? Why don't *you* take a stand?"

He swallowed a bite of food. "People know what I think," he said.

"It isn't enough."

"I'm just one person," he said.

"You're the pastor. You're in charge." Now the tears were spilling out. Somehow, I was able to keep talking.

"That isn't how it works," he said.

"How does it work?"

"We have a leadership team, voted on by the congregation. I'm one member of a seven-member team. Right now, that group isn't ready to make anything official."

"So what am I supposed to do?" Now I was really crying. Big fat tears rolled down my cheeks. My face was flushed, I'm sure.

He took a long breath. "At some point, you have to let go of what other people think. It's out of your control. Jesus said that in this world we will have trouble. And it's true." He held out his hands, as if to say, look at my broken body, wrecked with cancer—look at you, still living with a wound almost two decades old.

I stopped crying.

"It always comes down to the same thing," Darren said. "What do you believe? In whom do you believe?"

I got in my car and drove away. I pulled into my driveway, but I stayed in the car; the engine was still running. I couldn't even turn the keys. I just stared at them.

I was seventeen when I had my first girlfriend. She would come over to my house to study, and I didn't think my parents suspected a thing, until my mom barged into my room and found us sitting next to one another on my bed. We weren't kissing or anything, but she knew right away. My parents freaked and called the youth pastor. He showed up in his jeans and sandals and a backward baseball cap. I thought it was going to be a conversation, but he didn't really want to talk. He wanted to pray for me. He brought us to the living room, me and my parents, and my stupid-ass youth pastor, sitting on our nicest furniture, started trying to pray the gay out of me, like some sort of exorcism. I left the house, jumped in my car, and drove to the parking lot of an empty strip-mall. At first, I was just angry. I was so angry. And then I started crying like I'd never cried before.

My parents have come around. It took years, but they eventually left that church and went to an open and affirming Lutheran church. I found my own path. I felt confident in my faith, but I was in and out of churches. Nothing ever seemed to fit quite right.

I had been wronged, but I was never going to get an apology. Never. That, I realized, was what Darren had been trying to tell me. I picked up my phone, and for some reason, I thought of the bluegrass band Shelby and I had seen the night of our first date: Green Thunder. I found their album on Spotify and played it through the car stereo. I turned up the music and kept sitting there, listening as it twanged and jangled. I couldn't remember all the stages of grief, but I knew anger was in there—anger and denial. I wasn't exactly a psychologist, but I understood enough to know I was stuck. Stunted.

I turned off my car, took my keys, and walked into the house. I leaned back against the door. I texted Shelby and apologized for the way I'd been acting. "I have some issues," I said.

"You think?" she answered.

That week, on a Wednesday night, for the first time, I left Barred Owl completely in the hands of my staff and took Shelby back to the cidery in the mountains. There was no band this time, just a dozen people or so, music coming from a set of tinny speakers. The grass had grown long in the fields, readying for the first cut of the year. The night smelled like clover.

We were sitting across from one another at a picnic table on a patio of crushed stone. The sun was dropping, and it was doing this Vermont thing where the whole world turns purple, a deep shade of lavender. It starts with the sky and the mountains, and eventually the grass and even the buildings take on this purple tint. It's ridiculous.

"Did you know that the barred owl is stealing habitat from the great horned owl?" she asked.

"I read something about that." It had something to do with the diet of the great horn, which was more limited.

"Isn't our restaurant kind of the same way? Aren't we just putting someone else out of business?"

I took a sip of my cider. I thought about defending our restaurant, our barred owl. I could have said that it was like natural selection—that the restaurants that fail weren't healthy enough to survive. I could have argued that, ultimately, the competition was good for everyone. But I didn't.

"Humans are weird," she said. "We do the weirdest things."

I knew she was talking about me, but I figured it was a nice way to put it, to include the whole species in her accusation. "Nothing makes sense," I said. "It just is." I was thinking about restaurants, relationships, cancer. If we could go back in time, then life would be reasonable. We could learn something, go back, and fix it. Instead, the world kept moving forward without our consent. It never stopped.

Right then, while we were talking, we heard the owl, calling out, its voice rising over the music. It was so beautiful.

"It blows me away," I said. "It gets me every time."

Shelby laughed. "Suck it, great horn."

"Yeah," I said. "Suck it."

Skimming

IT WAS THE SAME TRIP her school district sent her on two years earlier—the same seven a.m. flight, the same hotel. She quite possibly sat on the same park-style bench, while she waited for the hotel shuttle to pick her up from the Orlando airport. There was a strong taste of karma in the way it worked out, the way it was happening again, two years later, almost to the day.

The district didn't typically pay for teachers to attend conferences out of state. Normally, you had to apply for grants and go through that whole rigmarole. But the first time she attended the conference, the district actually paid her freight. Without warning, the school's math scores took a significant dip on the NECAP (the state level math and reading assessment), alarm bells sounded, and Amy, the lead Math Specialist, was suddenly off to the national gathering for the Association of Mathematics Teacher Educators in Orlando. She asked her principal where the money was coming from—money she had been told repeatedly they didn't have.

"We'll work it out," Dr. Pettyway. said

Dr. Pettyway was a small woman with skinny limbs, thick-rimmed glasses, and unnaturally tanned skin. She smiled, as if it was a good thing that the school's finances were strategically opaque. She talked about making this a regular event, rotating which staff attended, but it never happened. The next year the district's NECAP scores rebounded, and the funding dried up. But Amy made friends on that first trip with the director of the AMTE, and Darlene asked her to come back to the conference as a presenter with the association paying her way.

At the very least, it was an opportunity to get away from the Vermont winter—away from everything, really—which is why she found herself back in Orlando, waiting for her airport shuttle, her carry-on sitting at her feet like a silent pet, texting her husband about the kids' schedule for the weekend. In a certain sense, Brian was a good father. He was caring and supportive. In other respects, he was useless. She was the one who managed the kids' schedules, made sure they ate healthy food and did their homework. When the kids were with Brian, she gave him detailed lists, and he would still drop the ball.

Her family life and work life were like parallel worlds. In both cases, she was the behind-the-scenes operator who made it all work, and in both cases, no one noticed. Of course, the cold hard truth was that classroom teachers were barely appreciated and specialists even less so. She had a bachelors from Wesleyan, a masters from Dartmouth. She had logged fifteen years in her field. She had even been a part of a research team that published a paper in the *International Journal of Science and Mathematics Education*. Despite all of that, she made less than half what Brian did. He worked for the largest marketing firm in Vermont and pulled down a good salary. In the past, it hadn't really bothered her. But lately, it was grating on her. Maybe it was because she and Brian were separated, and she worried about her financial future in a way she hadn't. Or maybe she was just sick of it.

The conference was taking place in the ballroom of a Marriott. Her room was on the seventh floor. As she rode the elevator, she looked at the schedule, surprised to see her own face, along with her bio, on the second page of the brochure. She was presenting on that research paper from graduate school. It was seven years old now, and she worried it was dated. Now that she was here, she wished she hadn't ever mentioned the project to Darlene. When the elevator doors opened, she hesitated before she stepped into the hall. By the time she entered her hotel room, she was sure it was all a mistake. All of it. Leaving home. Presenting at the conference. Becoming a math specialist. There were days—and lately they were more and more common—when, during the quiet moments, the rare pauses in her schedule, she thought about walking down to the principal's office and quitting. Just like that. And that would most certainly be the way she would do it. No letter. She wanted to see Pettyway's face when she said it: "I'm tired, I'm undervalued, and I'm doing this anymore."

She kicked off her shoes, pulled down the comforter, and dropped onto the bed. She looked down at her feet, wriggling her toes and watching the shape of her feet change inside her socks.

As she lay there, trying to relax, she thought about a news story from back home. A man from a small town near Burlington was caught by federal agents, charged with distributing child pornography. He was married but didn't have any kids, and Amy was thinking about the man's wife. The woman left him and moved back to the Midwest, where she had grown up. Probably, she was hoping she could leave it all behind her, but someone was sure to look her up on the internet and find out. The embarrassment would follow her, reappearing like a lingering infection.

Amy could have lounged on the bed for the rest of the day, but she wasn't the type to attend a work conference and skip the opening keynote. Two times in middle school, she won an award for perfect attendance, which came with a free game at the bowling alley. In high school, she developed asthma, so that came to an end, but she was still that same person, who did all of the things she was supposed to do: PTO, carpool, soccer games, lacrosse. There weren't many suburbs in Vermont, but she was the prototypical suburban mom for the twenty-first century in the Green Mountain State. She worked a thankless job, chauffeured her pre-teens to school activities and friends' houses, and circled back to pick them up again in their trusty Subaru. She grew vegetables in their large garden, pulled weeds, canned the fresh produce in jams and sauces. She packed lunches with food from the co-op, taking her own reusable containers with her to the store. The list went on.

There was a little bit of time before the conference started, and she decided to shower. She kept turning up the temperature, again and again. She always took hot showers, but even for her, this was hot. She wanted to feel it deep in her tissue. She wanted to fill the room with steam, until she was swimming in it.

As she dressed and applied her make-up, she was still talking herself into going downstairs to the conference. What she wanted was to lie in bed, order room service, and watch Netflix on her computer. But the other part of her—the rule follower—still won out most of the time. And she did make it to the opening session, standing in the back, while the plenary speaker talked, plowing through the disturbances that came with the late-arriving crowd: voices in the lobby surging every time the door opened, the whispered greetings that came with this particular type of reunion, the hotel staff's polyester uniforms making that zipping sound as they scurried around and their pant legs rubbed against one another.

There was a trick she used in situations like this when she was alone in a crowd: she looked for someone who looked like her. Tall, thin, long black hair, glasses, a serious affect. This was how she found Darlene, and it's how she found Nancy this time around. Years ago, she had come across an article about a research study, which suggested that humans are attracted to people who looked like themselves. She had been laughing about the story with Brian, who looked nothing like her. He was stocky and tow-headed, and it had seemed funny at the time. Later, though, it occurred to her that she had several friends who did look like her, who might even have been confused with her from a distance. Eventually, she accepted the premise.

It took her a couple of minutes before she spotted Nancy seated on the left side of the conference room, about half-way back. She appeared to be alone. Amy approached and took a seat, leaving one chair between them, and setting her purse on the open chair. When the speaker finished, she introduced herself. They chatted for fifteen minutes, while the room emptied, and then it was Nancy who suggested they go to dinner at Bacaros, the restaurant across the street from the hotel. Amy couldn't think of a good excuse not to, and the next thing she knew they were crossing the lobby together.

Bacaros was a regional chain, and even though people regularly walked across the divided highway from the hotel, there wasn't a cross walk. Amy and Nancy jogged to the median, paused for traffic, and then, when there was an opening, ran the rest of the way.

A short wall of brick outlined the front of the building—two feet high with a small ledge, planters stationed every seven or eight feet, holding a waxy sort of plant she didn't recognize. Right now, it wasn't flowering, but she imagined it would bring forth large blooms, drooping and tropical. Nancy was chatting, talking about her kids, and she didn't notice that Amy turned quiet as they entered the building, holding her breath when the hostess led them past the table—that same table in the exact same location—breathing out when they were led to a corner booth at least twenty feet away.

The restaurant was nice. The tables and chairs were made of red-toned wood and looked expensive. The tile floor was arranged in a diagonal pattern, and it looked like slate, probably not real stone but a good knock-off. There was a large aquarium imbedded in the wall between dining rooms, glowing in aquamarine, the fish shimmering as they wriggled through the water. Dozens of pendant lights hung, suspended from the open ceiling, a labyrinth of metal beams and ductwork, painted black. The food, on the other hand, was marginal. She ordered a chicken wrap, and the meat was overdone, the dressing runny and uninspired. She wondered if they were simply giving people what they wanted: form over substance.

Nancy said that she liked the opening speaker but complained that it was unrealistic. "I mean, it's great information, but when am I going to rewrite our entire curriculum? Who has that kind of time?"

"I know," Amy said. "I can barely keep my head above water."

"I don't want to complain," Nancy said. "Well, maybe I do." Her head bobbed when she laughed.

Soon, Amy was laughing so hard she had tears on her cheeks. "You have to stop it," she said, "or I won't be able to eat this shitty sandwich."

"Oh, what's wrong with it?"

"Nothing." She shrugged and looked over at the table again without thinking. It wasn't the first time she had looked over Nancy's shoulder.

"Are you looking for someone?"

She said she was looking at the fish. "They're just so pretty."

"I like fish," Nancy said. "Grilled and with a side of mashed potatoes."

"I think you're my soulmate," Amy said. And she did feel a sense of connection with this woman, though she knew little about her. Nancy had shared the names and ages of her children (Preston, seven, and Arthur, five), had offered up her husband's name and career (Trent, professor of entomology at Ohio State). She knew that they lived in a suburb of Columbus (Dublin), and of course that she was a math specialist. But that was it.

"I'm feeling nervous about presenting," she said.

"You'll do great." Nancy had her shoulder-length hair tucked behind her ears, and it stayed there throughout the meal, obedient.

"It's so strange," Amy said. "The whole thing. All of us here in one place."

Nancy's eyes were green and hazel, mixed together like spilled paint. "At the very least, it's a break," she said. "No cooking, no dishes, no errands. Everything else is gravy."

Back in her hotel room, Amy took out her laptop. She was planning on going over her presentation, but there was another document open, a script she had recently started for a play. It wasn't even a script, at this point, just a series of notes. She hadn't written anything in years, so even having an idea and a document—that was something. She added to her notes. One of the notes became a scene, or at least part of a scene, with a half-dozen lines of dialogue. But then she paused, unsure about the next line. Uncertainty turned into doubt, and she closed the computer.

She called Brian and said hi to Courtney, her thirteen-year-old, and then Dirk, who was ten and didn't know how to hide his confusion at his parents' separation. Even when he smiled, he looked like he might cry. After Dirk, Brian got back on.

"What did you have for dinner?" she asked.

"Oh, nothing special," he said.

"How not special are we talking?"

"Chicken strips," he said.

"Any vegetables?"

"Do tater tots count?"

"No, fried potatoes do not count as a vegetable." She was irritated but decided to let it go. After all, Brian was watching the kids, driving them every which way to their activities, so she could travel. When she hung up, she felt spent.

The first thing she ever stole was a wallet. It was sitting on that table at Bacaros, completely unattended, and, without thinking, she had reached out and grabbed it, and then stuck it in her purse. She'd had a few drinks, but that didn't explain the fact that she had done something so completely out of character. It was a new impulse, something she had never experienced in herself.

Inside the wallet was three hundred dollars cash. It was the wallet of someone on vacation—all of that cash, a hotel keycard, credit cards, and a bunch of receipts. She took the cash and left the wallet in the lobby of the hotel, tucked behind a seat cushion. A couple of weeks later, when she received the reimbursement check for her trip expenses, she cashed it, and then hid all of the money in the box with her father's ashes, one place she knew Brian would never look.

It was surprising how easy it was, once she opened her eyes to the possibility. Later that winter, she went as a chaperone with Dirk's class on a trip to the Flynn, the big old theater in Burlington. At one point, she went to the bus to fetch an aspirin from her purse and saw that another mom had left her wallet in her jacket. She could just see its edge sticking out of the pocket. She recognized the jacket, knew that the woman was well-off, and it occurred to her that there might be a lot of cash. There was. Several hundred dollars in all denominations. Amy took seventy-five, confident it wouldn't be missed. And as far as she was aware, it never was. The whole time the bus driver was sitting on the curb, smoking.

And then there was the day she went to her friend Donna's house to take care of their dog. Donna and her husband were away for an overnight, and Amy offered to stop by after work. She entered through the garage, let out the dog, a sheltie, filled its bowl with food and freshened the water. She found cash in three different places: stuffed into a bill rack in the kitchen, sitting on a dresser in the bedroom, and tucked into envelopes in the desk in the office. All told, it was around four thousand dollars, and she took four hundred, skimming off the top of each stack.

Now she had a methodology. She stole from people who had more than enough, and took a relatively small amount, knowing that no one would ever accuse her of stealing petty cash. She was a white, middle-aged woman, who didn't need the money. On top of that, she was goody-goody. She was the team mom for lacrosse; she never drank too much at parties. There was no way that anyone would believe she was a thief. She couldn't even believe it herself, which is why she hadn't told a soul, not even her therapist.

The next morning, she met Nancy outside the conference room, just before the first session. They each had cups of coffee, and Nancy offered her a quick, one-armed hug.

She was feeling anxious, but she talked herself down. She didn't present until two o'clock, and it wasn't like she was a plenary speaker. She was leading a breakout session. There were two other breakouts during that time slot, and by the afternoon of the second day, some people would choose to skip. She would end up with a group of thirty to forty, she figured, and when she thought about it that way, it didn't feel so overwhelming.

She settled into her seat, her purse at her feet, and the plenary speaker started discussing a new batch of research on personal learning plans. Immediately, her confidence melted away. The woman used terminology like a second language, and Amy struggled to follow the discussion. The speaker kept using the word, *moderator*, and for the life of her, she couldn't remember what the term meant, though she was sure she had used it in grad school.

Nancy suggested they go for coffee. "I mean, real coffee," she said. Amy claimed that she needed to go over her slides and excused herself. Instead of heading up her room, she found a side door and walked outside. It was a cool day for Orlando, in the 50's and breezy. She wrapped her arms around herself and stood behind a large pillar, listening to the traffic. She was cold, but that didn't explain why her throat felt tight. Soon she was digging for air.

Her first thought was that was that it was her asthma, resurfacing. But there was the tightness in her chest, like a belt cinched around her torso.

She bent over and kept breathing, digging and digging. Now there was a pain in her shoulder, and she was sure she was having a heart attack. She had her cell phone out, ready to dial 9-1-1, when, finally, the pressure started to relax, breath upon breath, until it passed.

She stood up straight, stretched her back, grateful for the

relief and certain that she needed to get away from the conference. She remembered that the hotel offered a shuttle to Disney Springs, and she went to her room to get her jacket.

Even in the morning of a cool and breezy day, Disney Springs was busy. It wasn't the throng of people that flocked here in the evenings after a day spent at the parks, but there were still people everywhere, walking with their heads turned. She drifted with the crowd, until she came to the Lego store. Outside the open doors were a series of giant Lego sculptures: the seven dwarves at their mine, a knight fighting a dragon, Buzz Lightyear and Woody in flight. The dragon and knight were most impressive. The dragon's head rose above the smaller knight, twenty feet off the ground, while the knight raised his spear in defiance. According to a plaque, it had taken over five thousand hours to build and consumed over a million of the little Lego bricks.

Inside, a wall of cylindrical bins held a myriad of Lego pieces: bricks of all colors, sizes, and shapes; heads with painted faces, a series of different hats, and little plastic toupees. And then there were the kits. Walls with stacks and stacks of kits for sale. Models of real cars—the Mustang GT, a Volkswagen Beetle, a Porsche 911. There was a model of the Neuschwanstein and the Hogwarts Castle from Harry Potter. And then were the Star Wars sets—the Millennium Falcon and Luke

Skywalker's X-Wing. Even though, at twelve, Dirk was out-growing his Legos, he would love the Star Wars stuff.

The kits were very expensive. Most of the Star Wars kits were over two hundred dollars, and if she bought something for Dirk, she would have to get something for Courtney, who would want clothes. She thought about stealing one. She didn't see any security devices on the boxes, and some of them were small enough to fit in her purse.

She walked to the X-Wing kit, sidled up to it. She could slide it into her purse. It was possible. But she stopped her-self. There would be security cameras, and there were a lot of employees, maybe a dozen of them, wearing yellow aprons and name tags. What if she got caught? How could she ever explain this? It was crazy. She was crazy.

She left the store, found an unoccupied bench, and sat down, facing a channel of water. The canal ran beneath arched bridges, along the manicured boardwalk. Her purse was on the bench next to her, and she felt for the iPhone she had taken from the airport. Stolen, really. It was during her layover at Reagan when she saw the phone at a charging station. No one was watching it. They must have gone to the bathroom or somehow forgotten it. It was a newer model, and she figured it was worth a couple hundred.

A flag pole rattled, banging angrily. The water in the lagoon rippled, shaking, as if in gestation. She felt dizzy and unbalanced. She still had a couple of hours before her presentation, but she couldn't imagine how she was going to stand up and talk.

A few minutes later a family of four walked by. The husband touched his wife's arm, and the girl, a young teen, walked in front of her brother, pretending she didn't see him and then stopped suddenly in his path. He walked straight into her, and they both laughed.

She had to regroup. She was hungry—that was part of the problem anyway. She stood up and started to move. She passed several shops and a street performer playing a saxophone. At first, she felt shaky, but eventually, she found her balance. She bought herself a hot dog from a food truck, something she hadn't eaten in years, since the kids were little. She ate the whole thing in a few large bites. Then she found a Starbucks and bought a coffee and leaned against the outside of the building, watching groups of people enter and leave.

It was apropos that she had chosen to hide away the stolen money with her father's ashes, though she had chosen the spot out of practical concerns. When her dad died, her mom gave some of the life insurance payout to her and her sister, and her portion went toward Brian's graduate school. He had just applied to the Harvard Business School, a total shot in the dark. He was accepted, and then her dad died, and then the money came through. She didn't blame Brian; it was a mutual decision. What she resented was the whole arrangement. As a wife, mother, and teacher, she was serving, serving, serving, and then living from the crumbs that were left on the table. But now she had something that was just for her, stowed away in that box. It didn't compare to the life insurance money, but it was something.

There was a little bit of sun now, and she was soaking in it, there against that brick wall, out of the wind. Eventually, she grew restless and decided to keep moving. On one side of the avenue, there were stores and themed restaurants. On the other ran the canal, a vault of dark water, huddled beneath the esplanade.

She ducked into a store—a big gift shop filled with Disney merchandise: t-shirts, hats, ornaments, coffee mugs, plush toys, and key chains. There were fairy wings, wands, and toy castles. None of it was particularly interesting. Her kids were too old, and they'd never really been Disney people. But then she saw something that caught her eye: a Euro Disney t-shirt with Mickey Mouse leaning against the Eiffel Tower. It wasn't Euro Disney that she was interested in. She couldn't imagine going all the way to France and then wasting time at a lesser Disney World. But Paris. The Loire Valley. Burgundy.

There was no reason to worry about her presentation. Her research might not have been the newest, but it was still relevant, and it was an easy crowd. These were her people, after all—the only people in the world who were thrilled to hear a lecture on a research study, comparing the math acuity of children who did and didn't know their multiplication tables. As soon as she started describing the experiment, someone said, "Oh, interesting." It was a cake walk.

After the presentation, she asked Nancy to meet her at Bacaros. She went back to her room, dropped off her computer, and touched up her makeup. Then she walked across the street.

"Here we are again," she said. They ordered from the bar and wandered over to the aquarium.

"I burned through that per diem the first night," Nancy said.

Amy was looking at the fish. There were two types—killifish with shining scales, splotches, and streaks of color, reds and oranges—and these little neon tetras, like children to the killis, darting between the much larger fish. In a huddle, the fish moved to one side of the tank, the tetras weaving between the larger killifish. Eventually, the tetras darted away.

"I'm thinking about calling Brian," she said.

"Okay." Nancy took a sip of her gin and tonic, and the little straw just missed her nostril.

"I haven't told him what I need. I always tell him that he's opaque, but then I'm like a brick wall."

"What do you need?" Nancy asked.

"Time."

"That's not very specific."

"Well, it feels outrageous. It's hard to say."

They walked back to the bar and hopped onto their stools. Amy ordered another glass of pinot noir.

"Try me," Nancy said. "Give it a test run."

"Okay." She took another sip of wine and then launched into it. She said that she wanted to leave teaching and become a playwright. She explained that she had some money saved and she wanted to go to France for a month, maybe two, write a couple of pieces, come home, and shop them around. In college, she was a double major—math education and writing. A play she wrote her senior year even won a competition. There was a cash prize, and a group of students performed her piece the week before graduation. It was all there for her, if she had made the choice: grad school in New York, a career in the arts. But then there was Brian, and they were going to get married. Teaching was so much more practical.

Nancy clucked. "I have this theory about people," she said. "I'm always telling Trent that people aren't what they seem. They never are."

They had both been drinking and thought they should order some food, deciding on a couple of appetizers to share: fried calamari and seasoned shrimp. It made her think of Brian, the idea that people aren't what they seem. After all the years of knowing him, married for fifteen of them, she never would have believed that she would get the call she received from the police in the middle of the night. Brian had gone to a New Year's Eve party with friends from work, left the party drunk with another woman, and crashed his car into a tree. None of it was like Brian, and maybe that was why she was able to forgive him. Of course, she was angry. She felt angry, betrayed, embarrassed, worried, afraid. But the anger didn't keep.

When Nancy went to the bathroom, leaving her purse on her chair, Amy picked out the wallet, unzipped and unfolded it, so that it was all right there in front of her: A couple hundred dollars in cash, a MasterCard and a Kohl's card, two Starbucks gift cards. There was plenty to skim off the top, but the urge wasn't there. Something was different now.

She was teary-eyed when Nancy returned.

"What is it?" Nancy asked.

"I don't know. Sometimes I feel like a rotten person."

"Oh, posh." Nancy put her hand on her shoulder and Amy leaned into it, soaking in the warmth of her friend's touch.

"You're a sweet woman," Nancy said.

Finally, when the sun had gone down, they left the restaurant. Brian would be getting home soon with Dirk from hockey practice. They would need some time to grab dinner. Most likely pizza. Then she would call.

The road was busy, headlights quivering in approach, and it took them a few minutes to cross the road. Nancy took off her heels, and when there was a short break in traffic, they made a dash for it. They were breathing hard and laughing as they entered the hotel, knowing that they had taken fate into their own hands and won a small victory.

"I guess this is it," Nancy said.

"Home again, home again," Amy said. She could see it now, the four of them together, forging onward, the silent past like a fifth chair at their table.

They embraced and Nancy turned away, heading off to her room on the second floor. "Bonjour," she called out as she entered the stairwell. "Bonjour, mon ami."

Something Worthy of His Shame

THE CONTROL ROOM OF THE steamship was always warm. In midsummer, the heat was oppressive. By the time Matthew had finished bringing the engine up to speed and locked the automator into place, synchronizing the flow of steam with the rise and fall of the cylinder, he was dripping with sweat. He mopped his forehead and traced his jawline with a handkerchief.

His fair skin was chapped from the hours spent in the belly of the ship amid the boiler's thrumming heat. His nose was crusted with dry skin. He had grown a beard, but the mustache didn't cover the patches of red worn onto his upper lip. He had tried every type of balm and oil to manage his psoriasis. Nothing worked. Being a ship's engineer was a cost to his appearance.

Leaving the control room, Matthew found Freddy, his assistant, reclining in the crew's cabin, resting his legs on a second chair. He was reading a *Life Magazine*, and Matthew could see the cover as he approached: a man and woman dancing, the woman's pearls flying.

"Okay then," Matthew said.

For a moment, Freddy didn't respond, and Matthew waited impatiently, strumming his fingers on his thighs. Freddy stood, tossing his magazine onto the chair in front of him. Most likely, Freddy would find some other distraction—visiting the toilet or passing a word with another crew member—before taking his place behind the controls. Matthew didn't believe his understudy would ever make engineer. He had tried, again and again, explaining to Freddy that the steam engine required vigilant attention, but the young man never seemed to grasp the gravity of his position. Perhaps Freddy was too used to things working out, incarnated as he had been into a well-formed body with perfect skin and rows of milky white teeth. Perhaps it was not possible for Freddy to understand what Matthew knew first-hand—that God is just as likely to make sport of his creatures as he is to provide for their needs.

Matthew slid the displaced chair back into its row, taking the seat Freddy had vacated. He removed a folded piece of paper from his coat pocket. Sunlight poked into the cabin through a small window, but the dark-paneled walls soaked up the light and the room remained dim. Still, he didn't have to strain to read the words; he had already read the letter several times, deciphering his uncle's looping cursive, and had it largely committed to memory.

"She is a hard-working lass and well-mannered. Truly, she is a lovely girl, and I'm sure you will find that her only defect is her thick Scottish brogue. Sometimes, even I can't understand her."

Matthew refolded the paper and tucked it back into his breast pocket, wondering again whether he shouldn't just go ahead and take the girl, though he was convinced that, in saying she was lovely, his uncle meant that she was gentle, not pretty.

Mary, the ship's stewardess, appeared at the door.

"Excuse me, sir," she said, "but a woman and her son would very much enjoy a tour of the ship."

Despite his self-conscious nature, Matthew didn't mind occasionally giving tours. He enjoyed showing off the *Ticonderoga*, built twenty years before with an engine from the Hoboken Ferryboat Company and a hull constructed in Newburgh, New York. At the Shelburne Shipyard, the top craftsmen in the state of Vermont went to work fashioning one of the finest vessels in the world.

"Just give me a moment," he said and walked to the toilet where he could inspect his appearance before heading above deck.

The woman and son were waiting on the balcony of the main

deck, standing at the railing. The mother looked out over the water toward Vermont, strands of loose hair playing in the wind.

Matthew had followed the same route around Lake Champlain hundreds of times, and he could almost feel the lake broadening as they traveled north along the eastern shore. There were four more ports in Vermont (Charlotte, Shelburne, Burlington, and Grand Isle) before the ferry crossed over to New York and turned south. In all, the journey covered almost one hundred miles and took a full day.

Matthew pictured the boat as it would have appeared from the shoreline. From that distance, the big white ship would have seemed oblivious to the wind and waves. The long double-decker would have appeared still in the water if not for the diamond-shaped walking beam teetering back and forth on the roof deck. On board, it was a different story. The boat rocked. Even high above the water on the main deck, he could feel the ship's hull driving against the water.

"Who are you?" the boy asked.

The mother turned around.

"I am the engineer for the *Ticonderoga*, and I will be your tour guide. If you'll have me."

"Certainly." The boy nodded

He was five or six years old, a year or two younger than his landlord's child.

"This is my son, Peter," the mother said. "And I'm Dorothy."

She was wearing a simple blue dress, decorated with buttons on the front and pleated below the waist. She was framed by the green Vermont hillsides and, further distant, the paisley mountains drawn zigzag across the bottom of the sky. She was the sort of woman that you noticed, not only for her beauty but for the way she held herself—straight and tall, as if she were always preparing to be photographed.

Matthew started the tour by heading down the stairs. When they reached the ship's bottom deck, he stopped in front of the business office. The office was cluttered with papers, tickets, and typewriters. Two men worked side by side, murmuring back and forth, filling the room with cigarette smoke.

Matthew looked down. "This floor is one of the ship's more interesting features," he said. The tiles were shaped like puzzle pieces, two inches long, thousands of them locked together into a pattern that seemed to go on forever. "These pieces were forged in a General Motors Auto Factory in Detroit—made from tire rubber."

Peter was watching the men in the control room, caught up in the sputtering activity. A voice, a pause, the click-clacking of a typewriter.

"Well, that is something," Dorothy said, looking down.

While her eyes were occupied, Matthew noticed how her torso gathered at a narrow, belted waist. She was not wearing a wedding band.

"I haven't introduced myself. My name is Matthew Bender." As Matthew offered his hand, he pictured his own half-hearted smile, the uneven beard and blotchy skin, misaligned teeth trying to hide behind thin lips. "What is your destination today?"

"We're going home to our farm in Port Douglas," she said. "At least it's home for now." She looked down at the floor again. "Peter's father died in the war, and we're living with my parents."

Matthew made a quick calculation. Her husband would have died three years ago, at least. If it wasn't for his gimpy left knee, Matthew might have died then as well. Two of his classmates froze to death in Hürtgen Forest, and he always assumed he would have died there also. Even though the war was starting to fade into the background of daily life, he couldn't seem to leave the guilt behind. The near-constant pain in his knee was his penance. He ended most days with his leg elevated, ice on his knee, grateful for the pain.

The control room was empty, and for once, Matthew was glad about Freddy's irresponsibility. He wanted to have the room to himself. Of course, just as Matthew was describing the ship's intercom, a pair of tubes and bells running from the control room twenty feet up to the pilot house, Freddy reappeared, as if smelling dinner about to come out of the oven.

"Young man," Freddy interjected, "do you want to ring the bell? We have a special ring that tells the captain we have a guest in the control room."

"Could I?" Peter asked, looking to his mother.

She smiled at Freddy. "How kind of you."

Freddy grabbed Peter by the waist and lifted him up so he could reach the bell cord. The boy's lips were pursed with focus as he grabbed the knotted rope. When Freddy set Peter back down, the boy was beaming.

"She's a beauty, isn't she?" Freddy looked at the engine and then at Dorothy.

"It certainly is impressive," Dorothy said.

"Impressive," Matthew said, "is closer to the mark. This engine is the result of decades of refinement, every component crafted with precision." Matthew had served aboard The *Ticonderoga* for nearly five years, but he still found himself occasionally pausing his work to admire the perfect curvature of the steel pistons, the grace with which the interlocking gears drove the ship's paddles, the massive force generated by a cauldron of boiling water.

"Yes, I can see that," she said.

Matthew led Dorothy and Peter out of the control room. They passed the stewardess's quarters, a private room for the ship's only female staff. For Matthew, this room was the ship's lone mystery, the world of the woman. They continued on to the bow of the lower deck, packed full with automobiles, horses, buggies, livestock, and three large storage bins of grain. The storage area smelled of wet leather, grass, and manure.

There was a persistent problem with mice, and he shuffled his feet, hoping any vermin would scurry away.

"It's like Noah's Ark," Dorothy said, smiling.

Peter approached a buggy, stepping on tiptoes trying to see inside. Cattle moaned from the other side of the deck.

Matthew was thinking about this young widow—how life had driven her back to the family farm while practically everyone else, it seemed, was moving to the city, leaving their parents and grandparents behind to tend the unwanted land.

"Is it lonely back on the farm?" he asked.

"Lonely might not be the right word."

"I'm sorry," he said. "I'm prying."

While Peter explored his surroundings, Dorothy leaned back against a wall made from rough, undressed pine. She held herself steady against the ship's rolling motion with the palms of her hands, and Matthew worried she would get splinters in her fingers or snag her dress against the bristly wood. The lower deck was rustic, unlike the passengers' cabins upstairs, which carpenters had lined with cherry wood, sanded smooth and lacquered.

Since he'd met Dorothy, Matthew had been careful with his eyes. But for a moment he allowed them to focus on her soft skin, tender pink lips, and the slope of her graceful neck. He imagined himself pulling back the collar of her dress, kissing the hollow of her shoulder. He thought about the long slender legs hiding beneath her ankle-length dress.

"Be careful, Peter," she said. The boy was right behind Matthew, approaching a gray pony tied to a metal beam. Peter stopped moving toward the animal. He lowered his hands.

"Do you live on board?" Dorothy asked, walking closer.

"Oh no," he said. "I have a place in Burlington."

"A place? That sounds lonely." She offered an impish smile.

Matthew didn't answer. He felt uncertain speaking with this woman, worried that the more he said the more likely he was to betray his clumsiness. He approached the pony, stroking its neck. The pony was chewing on some hay, folding it into his mouth, crunching and waggling its head. Matthew waved for Peter to approach, and the boy mimicked him, running his hand down the pony's neck to the withers.

He knelt down beside the boy. "Are you making friends?" he asked.

"Oh yes," Peter said. "The animals are all my friends."

Matthew smiled. If only he shared the boy's confidence, his certainty in the reciprocating affection of others. If only he possessed the sort of panache that allowed a man to speak to a woman, knowing that she would find him charming.

Leaving the busy storage deck behind, Matthew led his guests to the crew's cabin and then back upstairs to the lounge, busy with passengers. For a moment, he lingered. A breeze was flowing through the lounge, ruffling his stiff, matted hair.

"Thank you for the tour. It's a wonderful ship," she said.

"Oh, it is. And thank you. You were very gracious." He couldn't think of anything else to say.

The Village of Charlotte was a minor port, and they docked for only a few minutes as passengers boarded and disembarked the ship. Soon Matthew was again working the starting bar, bringing the engine back up to speed for the next leg of the northward journey to Shelburne. He was just about to set the automator when he saw Dorothy rushing past, her perfect posture ruined by an urgency of movement. He finished his work and went looking for her.

Dorothy was in the big storage room calling for Peter. When she saw Matthew, she said, "I told him not to leave his seat. I told him not to move a muscle."

"What happened?" he asked.

"I went to the restroom, and when I came back, he was gone." Her face was as white as the limestone cliffs at Rock Point. She seemed almost to have transformed into a different person. Her mannerisms were changed—her voice pinched with fear, her strides long and uneven as she walked across the storage deck looking for her boy. Peter could have been hiding any number of places. He could have sneaked into one of the buggies, though Matthew didn't see how he could have climbed into one of the grain bins.

"He doesn't know how to swim," she said.

Matthew could almost see her insides churning like the lake waters swirling below as she confronted the possibility that she had lost her son.

"He's a smart boy," Matthew said. "He's going to be all right, we just have to find him. And we will." He had never won a prize in his life, not even a spelling bee. With the condition of his knee, he had never participated in athletics. If he managed to find Peter, for once he might play the hero. Promising to find help, he went striding down the hall, up the stairs to the lounge, where he found Mary.

"I can't imagine where he could have gotten off to," the stewardess said, "or that he could have fallen overboard without being noticed." Mary's personality matched her body, solid and unwavering, functional but without grace. Matthew suspected that she was chosen for the job partly for her competence, but also because she would not distract the male crew.

"True," he said. "But the mother will be in a panic until we find him."

He asked Mary to help Dorothy search the lower deck, while he made for the pilothouse.

"If you see Freddy," he said, "send him back to the control room." Then he climbed the second set of stairs to the roof deck. He rarely visited the top of the ship, and it took a moment for his eyes to adjust to the harsh light—the shimmering sun reflecting off the water, the enameled deck, the gleaming white railings and flagpoles. In the sun and the wind, his eyes startled to tears.

Walking carefully across the rocking boat, Matthew wondered why he allowed himself to fantasize about women like Dorothy. In all his life, only one woman had expressed any romantic interest in him, a sad girl named Rose (he'd always thought of her as a girl, though she was nearly his age). She had worked in the boarding house where he lived five years before, back when he was ship's mate on a steamer running in and out of New York Harbor. She wore a black blouse beneath a plain white apron, the faded black cloth matching the shadowed hollows of her eyes, which always looked sunken in the dusky, lantern-lit house.

She had taken to him immediately, and for a few weeks, he had been flattered. She certainly wasn't beautiful, but she was pretty in the way a wilting flower becomes remarkably soft in its frailty. As time passed, though, Matthew grew more and more certain that he would turn the girl away. Part of him, deep inside, always believed that someday a woman like Dorothy would appear: tall and beautiful. It was the other part of him, however, that was speaking now, criticizing his desire for a woman he could never have.

The boy was nowhere to be found. The captain hadn't seen him on the roof deck, and Matthew did not find him in the restaurant or in either of the sleeping rooms. He descended to the lower deck, and, as he took the stairs, he felt his knee groan. Passing the control room, he raised his hand to acknowledge Freddy, who had, in fact, taken his position. Dorothy was still searching the storage room. Her eyes flashed with panic.

"He must have gotten off in Charlotte," Matthew said. "I'm sure he's sitting on the pier right now, waiting for the ship to return."

"He's gone," she cried. "I know he's gone." She leaned against one of the large grain bins, awkwardly resting her shoulder and neck against the bin.

Matthew wanted to reach out and hold her. She was a tall woman, but he was sure that he could lift her. He could pick her up and carry her away, her head resting against his chest. He could practically feel the electricity of her body against his. But it was an absurd thought. And, of course, he couldn't rescue her from the fear that was consuming her. The only answer was to find the boy.

She looked up at Matthew from her strange position. Her eyes were red, and her mascara had smeared, leaving a black streak on her cheekbone.

"What are we going to do?" she asked.

Matthew was sure again. The boy was not dead but had almost certainly left the ship in Charlotte. He knew what this was about. His parents were older and doting. They rarely punished him, and even when they tried, often failed to follow through. One time, he had broken a mirror, and his mother had sent him out of the house. He stood outside the kitchen window screaming, and crying, and banging against the side of the house, until his mother finally, guiltily, let him back in. Peter's disappearance, he was sure, was a cry for attention.

Matthew promised to help search the ship again as soon as he had checked in with his assistant. Introduced again to the extreme heat of the control room, it took only a few seconds before his armpits began dripping with sweat.

Freddy looked startled. "Matthew," he said, "I'm glad you're here." The pressure gauge had been moving upward.

"It's something to watch," Matthew said. It irritated him that Freddy, who couldn't be trusted to pay careful attention to the controls, was now worried about a slight increase in pressure, something that was quite normal on a hot summer day.

"You're not worried?" Freddy asked, mopping his brow with his handkerchief.

"Not yet," Matthew said.

The hallway felt narrow and cramped. He practically lived on board the *Ticonderoga* and was used to its tight spaces and low ceilings, but every once in a great while, the cramped lower deck felt small and bereft of air. The feeling put his senses on high alert. He could feel the heat coming from the engine room. There was a little scuffing noise in the wall separating the hallway from the stewardess's cabin, almost certainly a mouse scurrying from one hole to another. They were constantly setting traps but were never able to completely rid the ship of pests.

After searching the ship again, Matthew found Dorothy outside the dining room.

"I'm going to be remarried," Dorothy said. "I told Peter, and now he's acting out."

Matthew ran his fingers through his beard with one hand and checked his watch with the other. "Another reason to think that he left the ship."

Red blotches had formed on Dorothy's neck. Her eyes were bloodshot, and more hair had fallen out of its bun.

"Maybe you should sit down for a minute," he said.

"I should have waited," she said. "I should have known he wasn't ready."

Matthew returned to the control room, and he was alarmed by the heat. The steel pistons were shimmering. Streaks of blue shivered up and down the surface of the cylinders. The pressure was holding steady at 110 pounds. Freddy had repeatedly asked Matthew for a clear line—how much pressure was too much—and he kept explaining that running a steam engine was art as much as science. Gauges help, he would say, but they don't tell you everything.

Freddy's black hair was drenched with sweat, thick strands sticking to his forehead. His handkerchief was soaked, but he was still employing it, wiping his face like a windshield wiper throwing rainwater from glass. His jacket had been discarded, and his rough cotton shirt clung to his body.

Matthew stared at the engine. Below his feet, a storage tank trembled. He could hear the condenser hissing, cool lake water meeting the indefatigable steam.

"What do you think?" Matthew asked.

"She's running hot, no doubt about that," Freddy said.

"When we arrive at Shelburne, we'll empty the storage tanks and let the engine cool. It will put us behind schedule, but it's better safe than sorry."

"Captain will be up in arms," Freddy said.

"Schedule's a bitter mistress." He called the Captain on the intercom, delivered the news, and returned to the dining room.

Matthew felt silly for having assumed Dorothy was unattached. He was the type of person who felt he must always make an excuse for himself, as if his very existence required an apology. He wondered if the woman in the letter, the Scottish girl, felt the same way about the world, that her existence was some sort of cosmic mistake.

He ordered a glass of soda water and joined Dorothy at her table. He drank whiskey at home, but this was all he would allow himself on board.

"I'm terrified," she said. She was cupping her hands together, as if in prayer. Around the room, diners clinked silverware against dishes, oblivious to this woman's crisis.

He looked out the windows at the lake, wishing that the waves could stir up a fresh breeze. He needed relief—relief from the day's heat and from the anguish in Dorothy's eyes.

"You know what?" he said. "When we make it to Shelburne, I'll take you back to Charlotte."

"Oh, that would be wonderful." She took his hand. "You have been so wonderful."

When the ship was docked, Matthew and Freddy emptied the storage tanks. They covered their ears while the tanks screamed in relief. He told Freddy about Dorothy and asked him to guide the ship to Burlington.

"Be careful," Matthew said.

"You know I will," Freddy said.

Matthew felt encouraged by the earnestness in Freddy's voice. He led Dorothy onto the pier, carrying her suitcase a quarter of a mile to a filling station. Entering the garage, Matthew offered the man twenty dollars to borrow his car. "It's an emergency," he said. The man gave Matthew the key to a Ford Model T.

Dorothy was sitting on a little strip of grass lawn next to the road, her head buried in her knees. The sun was bright on the trees and glinting on little pieces of bauxite packed into the road. Matthew's knee ached. He had lumbered all over the ship, climbed the staircases repeatedly, and he knew he would pay for it later. He was headed for a poor night's sleep however things turned out.

The car had a rounded hood, a square grill on the front, and two chrome-plated headlamps that looked like eyes. The vehicle felt as out of place on those backcountry roads as a radio tower planted on the shaved top of a wild Vermont mountain. The top was down, and dust swirled all around the car. Throughout the drive, Matthew veered one way or another avoiding the biggest potholes. Still, the car banged and rattled, bouncing out of the biggest ruts.

For a while, Dorothy didn't speak, but then she said, "How much further?" She had taken her hair down and was trying to wind it back into a bun. She was holding the long hairpins in her teeth, and her hands remade the style with practiced ease.

"About four more miles, I'd say."

"Do you really think we'll find him?" she asked.

Matthew believed that he could now see into her mind. She was imagining what it would feel like to see Peter's form walking down the street, to call to him and see him turn toward her, and experience the beautiful recognition of the sweet child's face. She was allowing herself to feel, if only for a moment, the incredible relief in knowing that he was alive, as if she had the boy wrapped in her arms, and she was promising herself that she would never—never—lose him again.

"I really think so. Yes."

"Oh, God, I hope so."

Matthew drove the car as fast as possible on the rough road. He thought about the *Ticonderoga* steaming north, while he was traveling in the opposite direction. He reminded himself that Freddy had been apprenticing for well over a year now, but his mind kept running through the things that could go wrong—a broken safety valve, water loss, corrosion in the boiler. He thought about Rose and how he had lied to her, telling her that he was engaged to be married.

Charlotte was just a village: a dozen large white colonials, a general store known as the Brick Store, a congregational church, a doctor's office, and a firehouse. Matthew checked the Brick Store first, entering ahead of Dorothy, walking past the woven baskets filled with bright vegetables: tomatoes, peppers, and onions—and two shelves filled with canned goods. There were three patrons in the shop and a girl working behind the counter. Dorothy approached a middle-aged woman, asking if she had seen a six-year-old boy, walking alone. Matthew walked to the counter where two men were talking. No one had seen Peter.

They traveled down to the dock where a man was fishing from the pier. His canvas pants hung over the heel of his boots where they were muddied and frayed.

"We're looking for a boy," Matthew said. At first, the fisherman didn't turn but continued looking out toward the water. For a moment, Matthew thought he could see the line flying out from the end of the pole.

"He's six years old," said Dorothy. "We stopped here on the ferry, and we think he might have got off." Her chest was heaving, and she had to force the words through caught breaths.

The man turned. He was sunburnt on the top of his bald head. A bushy mustache covered most of his mouth. He pinched his lips to one side. "A boy," he said, "let me see."

Dorothy's eyes lit with anticipation. If the man had even seen Peter, at least she would know that he was alive. But then, as if the wind had suddenly shifted directions, and he had caught a different scent, the man tipped his head to the side and shook it.

"I haven't seen any children." He flashed an awkward smile, his teeth bared behind his mustache.

Returning to the village, they came up behind a roan horse, trotting along. When they came closer, they could see that there was a child seated behind the rider, close to Peter's age. Matthew drove alongside the horse until he could catch a glimpse of the child's face. It wasn't he.

Matthew drove into town and pulled the car off to the side of the road. He hung his jacket over the seat back behind him. His pants were sticking to his legs. Patches of sweat grew under his arms and in the center of his chest.

Dorothy's eyes darted around, unwilling to rest.

"I don't think he's here," Matthew said.

Dorothy broke into tears. She pounded the dashboard with the bottoms of her fists. "Dammit, Peter. Where are you?" The distress was crushing her now. Matthew could almost see it—the pain and anger like an aura radiating from her body.

He placed a hand on her shoulder, and her body settled back into its seat. Her eyes were closed, and he could feel her body rising and falling with each breath. It occurred to him that, for the time being, he was the only thing she had in the world. Peter was gone. This man to whom she had pledged herself was nowhere near. Matthew could imagine himself with her, some day in the future, walking arm and arm down the brick streets of Burlington, the city lights reflecting off the storefront windows, peeking into alleys. It wasn't impossible. If they found Peter, or even if they didn't, she would need someone like him, who was strong and capable. Someone to see her through.

They decided to drive to Burlington in an attempt to catch up with the *Ti*. For the first part of the drive, Dorothy didn't speak.

Her eyes were set straight ahead, though Matthew suspected that she was seeing only Peter. They passed open pasture where cattle and sheep huddled next to fences and rocks for the little shade they offered. They passed stretches of timber, hemlock tucked beneath the top-heavy white pine.

After they'd driven past the filling station in Shelburne, she said, "What if he's lost? What if I never see him again?"

"You can't think that way," he said.

"People die, Matthew. It happens. It happens all the god-damned time." The road became smoother as they approached Burlington, and the car was cruising along nicely. "I don't know. I don't know anything anymore." She took a big, gulping breath. "I was just starting to feel like a person again."

Burlington was alive with the traffic of cars, horses, and people. As they crossed Maple Street, he could hear the black-smith's hammer tolling like a muffled bell. Down the street, artisans worked in their shops. A cobbler, a potter, a man who dipped candles and carved wooden utensils. The city streets were rank with the smell of steaming manure, the sour burn of rotting hay.

He turned down King Street heading toward the harbor. This street was lined with yellow apartment houses, rambling structures that sheltered the men who kept the city's industry greased and moving forward—the dock workers and the ship builders, men who worked in the back rooms of restaurants,

who maintained the rail line, running south to Albany and
north to Montreal. The house where Matthew boarded was
two blocks away on a quieter street, but these, he felt, were his
people—these lonely men with blistered hands and feet, men
who drank away their evenings and their Sundays at the tav-
erns or, as in Matthew's case, the quiet of their own bare rooms.

Long before they reached the bay, Matthew could tell that
something was wrong. One man yelled to another across the
street, "Did you see?" "A shame," the other yelled. It might
have been nothing, but Matthew could feel the pulse beating in his temples. Their view of the waterfront was obscured
until they reached Battery Street and were running along a
few hundred feet above the lake. They passed the busy railroad station and then came into full view of the Burlington
Harbor. A large pile of coal stood like a black pyramid. Behind
the coal pile, stood the Electric Power Plant with its triple
smokestacks. The *Ticonderoga* was approaching the breakwater
and the sullen water of the harbor. The gallant steamship was
leaning hard to the port side, dragged along by a tug. The ballast must have been leaking, and the whole thing was ready to
topple over. He could see smoke billowing from the cabin. A
fire was burning below decks; almost certainly, it would have
started in the control room.

Four lifeboats had arrived at shore, and survivors were
being led away from the dock. A few were sprawled out in the

grass. Others stood around the waterfront like buoys leaning to one side or another, watching the scene.

As soon as Matthew parked, Dorothy ran from the car. "What happened? Has anyone seen my son, a little boy? His name is Peter."

For a moment, Matthew was frozen. His only thought was that this—all of this—was his fault. Whatever had caused the engine to overheat, if he'd been on board, he would have caught the problem in time. He stumbled out of the car, following Dorothy.

She was searching the waterfront, breaking up groups of onlookers.

"Yes," he heard someone say. "Over there."

And there, in fact, was the boy, Peter, sitting with Mary. She had found him in her cabin, underneath the bed. They were above decks when the engine overheated. He hadn't suffered a scratch. Later, Matthew would realize that Peter was, in fact, the mouse in the wall—that he had heard the boy hiding in the one place he never would have looked. At the moment, though, he was thinking about Freddy.

"He survived," Mary said. "I can tell you that much."

Freddy had fled the engine room before the fire started. As far as Mary was concerned, the incident revealed the apprentice's true colors: Instead of saving the engine, he fled. She had seen him racing toward a lifeboat when he fell, and was nearly trampled by a rush of passengers. When he finally reached shore, he was taken to the hospital with a broken arm, caused by his own panic.

Matthew felt sick, but nothing came. He saw the captain and the rest of the crew on the large dock, moving the lifeboats. Two fire engines awaited the Ticonderoga's arrival. He walked back to the car and sat in the driver's seat with the door open and his legs hanging out. He buried his head in his hands, and Dorothy came around and knelt before him, placing a hand on the top of his bad knee. The knee was swollen and tender, and even this kind gesture caused him pain.

"I will never be able to thank you enough," she said. She was shaking her head to confirm her belief. No, there was no way she could find the words or the gesture to fully express her gratitude.

It was the moment he had hoped for when all of this started. But now, he felt only regret. He kept thinking of the pulsing heat, shivering up and down the steel cylinders. The ship was speaking to him, and he wasn't listening. He was too busy chasing a woman—a woman who would never settle for a man like him. Not in a million years.

After a few minutes, he drove home. It wasn't far, but his knee was already swollen. The plaster in his room was darkened from years of dust and grime. Holes in the walls were patched carelessly, and he looked at these strange shapes while he waited. He knew when the train was due to arrive, leaving two hours to sit in his room. He drank whiskey and threw it up. He gathered a few things that were worth packing, including a silver framed picture of his parents at the Ohio farm, taken the year before they died, his mother from meningitis and his father, not long after, out of grief. He also packed his watch and some clothes: two of his best shirts and a pair of leather boots. The letter was sitting on the nightstand, damp from sweat, the ink blotted. He picked it up, tore the letter in half, and then in half again, letting the pieces fall to the floor.

He considered heading west. There were jobs in Idaho and Montana, harvesting forests for the rush of post-war construction. Even though his knee wouldn't allow hard labor, he was confident he could find a job. But no.

When he left his room, it was dusk. Streetlamps cast long shadows on the grass and dirt. The world felt hard beneath him as the Model T rolled down Maple Street toward the waterfront. The train station sat just above the harbor, and he could see the top deck of the *Ti* still holding its head above the water.

When he lived in the boarding house, he had turned ill, feverish and disoriented, and Rose had cared for him, replacing one cold wash cloth after another, coaxing him again and again to take a sip of water. Quietly and persistently, she had cared for him, though she believed he was engaged to another. Looking back, he realized that he never should have rejected her. It was his pride. Despite all of the shame, he was full of pride. Somehow, the two things lived together in him, intertwined.

He bought his ticket for New York. He had left a note for his landlord, asking that he return the car to Shelburne. He paid his rent and a little extra. He had a single bag. Sitting in the passenger car would make the swelling on his knee even worse. By the time he arrived in New York, he would be lucky if he could still walk.

The era of the steamship was ending. All the new ships were built with combustion engines. Steamship engineers were going extinct. The *Ti* would never be rebuilt. If it was replaced, it would be with a modern ship with a diesel engine. It would run quietly and efficiently, and without supervision.

Of course, Rose might be gone. Possibly she was married. She might not forgive him when he told her the truth. But there was something about the way the train was running, clicking over the tracks, lurching now and then, screeching to a stop when they came to Rutland and Springfield, that made him certain he was traveling in the right direction. It was a new diesel-electric. There wasn't the drive or the force of the steam engine. But it was steady. Even. Eventually, he dropped off to sleep, and when he woke, they had reached the outskirts of the city, just a few miles from their final destination.

World Upside Down

AT MICHIGAN STATE, WE CALLED ourselves the Crew. Not particularly original, I know. But to us, it meant something. We were non-affiliated (non-Greek) purveyors of fun. Basically, we were up for whatever shit was going down, and if nothing was going down, we made something happen. That was the first part of the Ethos, which was the essence of the Crew. We lived life hard. We sought adventure. The second part of the Ethos was that we took care of one another, though I'll be honest in saying that Kyleigh was the one who really took care of everyone else. Kyleigh was the one who lived the Ethos and gave us our name. Without Kyleigh, there was no Ethos and no Crew.

Kyleigh was always different. She officially formed the Crew sophomore year. By then, we had access to alcohol through Derek (a 22-year-old junior) and a party house. Kyleigh's parents are loaded, and they bought her an off-campus house, where she lived with her best friend, Sara, and a couple other girls.

Out of all of us, Kyleigh had the least at stake. Her parents had money, and I mean serious money. I think she felt guilty about that, which is at least part of the reason she did the whole thing at Shain Park. But I'll get to that in a minute. Point is, she could have coasted. My dad is an auto mechanic, and I paid for my own degree in construction management. Well, borrowed for my degree. But Kyleigh was really into her classes. Sometimes, you could tell that she was deep in thought, even while we were walking to the Quality Dairy to load up on booze. She was a sociology major, and that was a different sort of education. It was about learning to think, about understanding the world. She would go on these rants about things, about everything that was wrong with our society: structural racism, the corruption in our political system, all of the shit that women go through in our society. Yeah, I heard it all.

Despite everything I knew about Kyleigh, though, I was shocked when I saw her in the news.

It was two years since graduation, and we were still in touch, still hanging out. It was summer, and we spent weekends at her parents' place, hanging at the pool and drinking White Claws. They have this ridiculous set-up with two pools side by side: a four-lane lap pool and then another pool that's even bigger, curved, with a diving board on one end, and a big slide on the other (which is amazing when you're high—just saying).

There were a couple of things that seemed different about her that summer. She was running a lot for one thing. She did a 10k, was signed up for a half marathon, and was throwing around the idea of running a full. I don't know the right way of saying this without sounding like an ass, but she had always been a little bit heavier. She wasn't fat, but she wasn't thin either. Big boned. That's probably the less shitty way of saying it. So I just figured the exercise thing was a gambit to lose a few pounds. And maybe it was. But she was also taking action. She was moving.

And then there was what she was reading. I brought a novel to the pool with me most of the time, usually a Brad Thor thriller. She had always been into heavier stuff. I don't remember most of the authors, but I remember Roxanne Gay and some guy whose name sounded like Lip Shits. But now she was reading the Bible. Poolside. When I asked her about it, she said Jesus was the greatest moral philosopher in human history, that Gandhi and Martin Luther King were both inspired by Jesus, and maybe I should get a copy. I do have one. I just don't consider the Bible a summer beach read.

What bothered me is that she didn't tell me about it. Clearly, she had been thinking and planning. In the construction world, everything is about planning and sequencing, and so I know that things like this take time. She got a permit from the city of Birmingham, a swanky Detroit suburb where she was living with her parents, and she built the huge sign and standing board (that's what she called it in the newspaper—her standing board). This was something she had been thinking about, probably for months. And the whole time not a peep, not a word. I find out when my friend forwards me an article from the Oakland Press, and I'm like, what the fuck?

I saw the article when I was at a job site. I was waiting for the electrician to show. The homeowner wanted to change the placement of a switch and add an extra outlet in the kitchen island. I was planning on walking the electrician through the changes, but when I saw the article, I bolted. The construction site was way out in Milford, following the city's never-ending movement to the north and west, away from itself, so it was a good forty minutes before I parked my truck, pulling within a foot of the Mercedes in front of me. Asshole would be lucky if he could get out.

At first, I didn't notice anything unusual. The park was clean. White sidewalks contoured the green grass. The grass was lush, carefully trimmed, the strange mixture of natural and unnatural in a perfect lawn. The bandstand was empty, the park benches full.

Kyleigh was in front of the Freedom Sculpture. There was a small crowd gathered around her, but I could still see her.

She was standing on her head on one of those blue wrestling mats. Her body leaned against the standing board. Her arms braced like trusses.

I lingered in the back of the crowd. I knew from the article that she was standing on her head for five minutes out of every hour, and she was going for twelve hours every day. From eight to eight. For a couple of days, she left her standing board and sign up overnight, but kids vandalized it, leaving her spray-painted messages: *Blow Me* (written upside down, which was kind of funny) and other vulgarities, so she started bringing it home every night and setting it back up every morning.

The standing board was eight feet by eight feet, two sheets of plywood painted black and supported by some two-by-fours on the reverse. It was positioned in front of the Freedom Sculpture at the center of the park, but it only covered the bottom of the towering sculpture: two bronzed figures, male and female, flying away. She would tell me later that it was intentional, juxtaposing herself against the sculpture. While the two figures reached for the sky, backs arched, as if they were about to take flight, she was stuck to the ground, gravitationally fixed to this planet and its set of problems.

There was also a sign in front of the standing board. At the top, it said, "World Upside Down." Below was a chalkboard where people were writing things that they wished were different about the world, and unlike the vandals, people were taking this seriously. That first day I arrived on the scene, it was eleven in the morning, and it was already covered with words and phrases: "people starving, war, living wage, racism, distorted food system, bad teachers." I loved the last one. I imagined some pissed off third grader letting it rip.

Someone was counting down the time. Ninety seconds. Sixty seconds. I moved closer, and it's the weirdest thing, but when a person is upside down, you can't read their eyes. I didn't know if she saw me, until she was upright. She got down from her standing board with a flip, stood up, and this guy who was counting her down held her shoulder while she steadied herself.

There was a line of admirers, and she dealt with each one, while I waited on the side. It was twenty minutes before I got her attention.

"Wow," I said. I'll admit, it was a little sarcastic.

"See? That's why I didn't tell you."

"All that time, sitting at the pool, and not a word."

While we were arguing, Shoulder-boy was still hanging around. He was behind the standing board but visible, like a kid who's terrible at hide and seek. He was one of those guys with long hair, who's chronically tucking it behind their ears.

Kyleigh took a breath. "I didn't tell you, because I didn't want you to talk me out of it."

"Why would you think that?"

"Because I know you."

"Well," I said. "Maybe you don't."

There was this thing that happened senior year, a couple of months before graduation, and it was still hovering over our relationship. It was like when moisture gets between two panes of glass, and there's no way to get it clean.

It had been brewing for a while, at least for me. The more I got to know Kyleigh, the more attractive she became. She didn't perfectly fit our contemporary concept of beauty, but she was pretty. And smart. And kind. If you needed help with something, or if you were having a hard time, she was the first person you called. And I know that kindness might not sound like the sexiest thing in the world, but it kind of is.

The thing is, I didn't know how to tell her. With friends, the stakes are higher, and I just kept putting it off, until one night when we were both drunk. I know, super classy. The sad part is, even then, I didn't really say anything. I didn't declare myself. We were sitting next to one another on this old sagging couch, and we were basically falling into one another, hip to hip, laughing, and drinking. It was a warm day, and the crowded house kept getting hotter and hotter. Finally, she took my hand, and we walked to the porch. She hopped onto the railing, so we were face-to-face, and I leaned in and kissed her.

In the morning, I was hung over. My head ached. But

that was nothing compared with the awkwardness. Kyleigh was embarrassed. She got dressed under the covers. She barely said a word.

Walking home, I started getting angry. I would have understood if she would have said, "Hey, that was great, but I just want to be friends." But she was acting like it was the biggest mistake in the world—like *I* was the biggest mistake in the world.

I don't know why my reaction to her is to get angry, but with Kyleigh, that's where I go. So when I left Shain Park, I was pissed. I was mad that she didn't tell me what she was planning and mad that she was right—I would have tried talking her out of it. And if I'm really going to bare my soul here, the truth is I was jealous. I was jealous of Shoulder-boy and everyone else who was receiving her attention. And I was mad at myself for being jealous. I was a big old soup of mad.

The whole thing started really taking off the day I came to see her. Later that day, a TV news crew came and interviewed her. They showed some video of her standing on her head, caught her popping Advil (this was how she was dealing with the headaches and later on, the neck pain, the shoulder pain, the back pain), and did a conversation piece.

She was articulate. She said that what she was trying to do was to get people think about their lives. "More than anything else, World Upside Down is about getting people's attention," she said. "I want to shake people up. I want them to look at their lives differently—to take a different vantage point." She talked about how we so often follow the path of least resistance, like water running downhill, but that she has felt challenged, from reading about Jesus, to live a different kind of life.

Of course, they interviewed Shoulder-boy as well. Turns out his name is Ash, and he carried on about Kyleigh and how he had found her when he was at rock-bottom from a drug addiction. It was a great story, I guess, but I still wanted to punch his stupid face.

Online, people did what they do. There were a lot of people praising Kyleigh, but there are always haters. They said she was doing it for attention. Some people attacked her because she said Jesus was a great moral teacher, and they took offense. *You're wrong. He's the Son of God.* And then there were the guys making their guy-comments. Either she was hot or fat. Or both. A bunch of ass hats.

And maybe this is why I didn't vibe with what she was doing: because I didn't really think of people as fixable. They are what they are. Sure, there are people like Kyleigh, who actually think about things and actively seek to live good and meaningful lives. But those are few and far between. Most people simply don't care. You can give them all the information in the world, and they're still going to shop at Amazon and throw their plastic in the trash—they're going to idle their car while they sit in the drive-thru pumping more and more carbon into the atmosphere as they wait for the burger and fries that will give them diabetes. Because the thing they want, more than anything else, is comfort.

I couldn't stay mad at Kyleigh. When I saw some of the things people were saying about her online, I texted her and told her not to read the comments. Things were busy at work, and I was driving all over the Detroit area, hitting job sites from Dearborn to Dexter, but I still found time most days to stop by Shain Park and bring her a cup of coffee. She was a total iced coffee addict, something Shoulder-boy didn't know about her.

That Saturday, when I showed up with coffee, she said I was a life saver. She kept blinking while we talked. I could tell she wasn't doing great. It was hot. We were into the low nineties, and it was worse on the pavement where she was still setting up for World Upside Down. It was mid-day, so her standing board wasn't offering any shade, and we hid under a nearby tree. A breeze kicked up, which made it tolerable.

"How much longer are you going to do this?" I asked.

"As long as it takes." She blew the damp hair out of her face.

"To accomplish what?"

"I don't know. To feel like I've done something, like people have heard me."

She was wearing her standard Upside Down outfit: three quarter length leggings and a t-shirt tied in a ball at her waist. Her hair was a mess.

"I'm just worried about you," I said. "And I don't understand how this ends."

She lectured me about how it wasn't supposed to be easy. She had gone into this project knowing that it was going to be uncomfortable, and she wasn't going to stop because it was hot. It was summer. It was supposed to be hot. I told her to drink lots of water and not to push it too far. She said, "I am," and we left it there.

That afternoon, I had a shit-ton of work to do, so I stayed at a coffee shop in Birmingham and banged out a bunch of emails. I was behind on everything, partially because we were over-committed, and my subcontractors were over-committed—and it didn't help that I was zipping off to Shain Park every day to watch my best friend stand on her head.

Anyway, afternoon turned into evening, and I walked over to this great Mediterranean place for falafel. It was while I was eating my dinner that I got a call from a local Birmingham number. I don't normally answer calls from numbers I don't recognize, but I picked up. It was Kyleigh's dad. He was worried.

"There's this whole Upside Down thing," he said, "And honestly, she was acting different before that."

"I did notice a few things," I said. I had just finished eating, so I threw my wrapper in the trash and started down the street, passing Birmingham's line of upscale restaurants, boutiques, and jewelry stores. Now that the sun was dropping lower in the sky, it was almost pleasant to be out walking.

That's when he started talking about how she had mental health issues. "You know how she would sometimes disappear during college," he said.

"Yeah. I did notice that."

He said that she struggled with anxiety and depression. They had worked hard to keep it in check, but Kyleigh always had a mind of her own. "Do you understand me, Ryan?"

"Sure," I said. I had figured some of that out on my own—the depression piece, for sure—but, of course, I didn't know the extent of the issue.

Mr. Patterson asked me to talk to her. He said that he and Kyleigh's mom had tried having a conversation, but she shut them down.

"I mean, I'll try," I said.

"Thank you," he said. "That's all I ask."

This next part of the story is a little embarrassing. I decided to wait and follow her when she left the park. Creepy as hell, I know, but the call from her dad made me feel like I had permission. Someone needed to figure out what was going on, though I'll admit, what I really wanted to know was whether she was meeting Ash.

It wasn't the easiest subterfuge to pull off. In Michigan, it stays light forever in the summer, and I was driving my work truck with the name of the company, VanDyke Builders, on both sides of the vehicle. I really had to keep my distance, and right off the bat, I got caught at a traffic light while her white pickup truck went sailing through. But then I got lucky. She hit the next red. Plus, with her standing board strapped to the bed of the truck, she was pretty easy to see.

She pulled onto Woodward, the main drag through Birmingham, and I thought we might be heading out of town. But then she turned into a strip mall and walked into a Mexican restaurant. I was on lookout for Ash, but soon she was walking back to her truck with a bag of takeout. When she pulled out of the parking lot, she headed back where she came from. She wasn't leaving town. She was going back to her parents' place—probably to eat her dinner and go to bed.

I drove home to my third-floor apartment in West Bloomfield. I was pretty tired, but I decided to sit on my little balcony and watch the sunset. I poured myself a couple fingers of bourbon. Neat because ice was for sissies.

I felt pathetic. Here she was doing something good, something she believed in, and the best I could do was bring her a cup of coffee. And even that had an ulterior motive. There was a party in one of the other units, and I heard the music whenever the patio door opened and disappear when it shut. Eventually, the party ended, and the crickets took over, chirping like mad, filling the empty space.

The second week of World Upside Down is when the protests started. It started on Sunday, but I wasn't there. I was visiting my family back in Vicksburg, which is about an hour and a half away. Friends of my parents live on a lake down there, and we spent the day on the boat. We drank some beers, cranked some classic rock, and generally pretended like we were back in the aughts. Living light. I got home late. Probably shouldn't have driven.

While I was wasting away at my parents', Kyleigh was at Shain Park. She was counting down from her one o'clock stand, when people from this super conservative church showed up. She was getting down from her head stand, a process that was increasingly laborious. Instead of flipping onto her feet, she basically crumbled to the ground. Then she pulled herself up, climbing to her feet, trying to collect herself. The church people were already getting into her face, even though she was still dizzy, still leaning against the standing board. They demanded she repent. They said that her outfit was lewd, and she was stealing God's glory, whatever that means. They were angry that she had called Jesus a great moral teacher. She said that a woman had tears in her eyes when she called it blasphemy.

Kyleigh tried explaining herself. She said she loved Jesus. She said she didn't know if Jesus was the son of God or not—that she hadn't figured that out for herself—but she wanted people to know about his life and teaching. But she also said she had a mission, and she wasn't going to back down.

On Monday, when I brought her coffee, there was a double protest going on. The religious people were protesting Kyleigh, and now Kyleigh's supporters were protesting the protesters. Ash had joined Kyleigh at the standing board.

It turned out that the real issue for the church people was that they couldn't get permission from the city to set up a nativity in Shain Park, and here was Kyleigh doing her thing right in front of the Freedom Sculpture. When I arrived on the scene, a journalist was telling her that the church had filed a complaint with the city and were threatening a lawsuit. They had a lawyer from one of those religious law groups, the Alliance Defending Freedom. These are the people who defend bakers who won't make cakes for gay weddings.

"You're going to want to lawyer up," he said.

Kyleigh was tired. I could see it in her eyes. She was rolling her neck around.

"I have a permit," she said.

"Hey, you can do what you want," he said, "but, personally, I wouldn't want to see these assholes win."

When the journalist was gone, I moved closer. "I mean, your dad's a lawyer," I said.

"My dad isn't going to help me." She looked past me when she said it, like she was talking to someone behind me.

I had to leave for work, but I came back later that day. It was seven in the evening, her second-to-last stand of the day, and there was a big crowd. The protestors had gone home, unwilling to keep pace with Kyleigh's commitment, but I was able to hide behind her group of supporters. I walked up to the chalkboard. It was mostly empty, so I had plenty of room to write the words, *I believe in you.* Then I found a space where I could see Kyleigh through the crowd. They were counting down, as she struggled to the finish. Her hands were spread wide against her wrestling mat, balancing her body. Her arms were shaking.

Most of the Crew was now out of state. Sara was down in Indianapolis, a five-hour drive. Derek was still around, working for an investment firm downtown, and doing pretty well for himself. He said he was busy, but he offered to shift his schedule around and spend some time at the park. Between me, Derek, and Ash, we tried to make sure that one of us was hanging around Kyleigh as much as possible.

We texted back and forth about our schedule and how Kyleigh was doing, and it was a good thing, too, because the heat kept coming, and the protestors did, too. Each five-minute stand was an ordeal. Kyleigh needed help getting up and down from her standing board. One time, there was no one there except an old lady, who was walking her dog, and Kyleigh later admitted that the whole scene was ridiculous with this poor lady trying to hold onto her feet while she flailed and kicked.

In the mornings, she did okay, but in the evenings, after a long day in the heat, working the standing board, it was an adventure. During her last couple of stands, her arms would shake uncontrollably. She looked like she was fighting an earthquake. I hated watching, but I needed to keep my eyes on her in case she fell.

The hardest part was calling her dad. But sometimes we have to make compromises, even when we're doing the right thing. Even when we're sure it's the right thing.

It was around ten that night when her dad texted me, letting me know that she had gone to sleep. He left the garage door open. I had the tools I needed. After all, I worked for a construction company.

I snuck into the garage and, as quietly as possible, loaded the standing board onto the bed of my truck. I used a couple of tie-downs, cinching the board tight, and then I drove back to the shop.

I unscrewed the legs, and I could feel the tension unwind in my body. It was the right decision. There had been a death threat. Derek overheard the police telling Kyleigh about it. The police weren't too worried; the threat wasn't specific, just more screaming into the internet. But when Derek texted me and Ash, I knew what I had to do. As I tore through the standing board with my skill saw, I cut straight lines, ripping the plywood into long strips.

I threw the wood into the bed of my truck and brought it back to her garage, so she would know. It was over.

Kyleigh was mad, and I can't blame her. The next morning, she called me while I was driving to the office.

"Was it you?"

I had planned on just telling her straight up, but I hesitated. I was holding on the bottom of the steering wheel, casual-like.

"Ryan?"

I sighed. "Yes."

She hung up.

It was a month before she would communicate with me again, two months before I saw her in the flesh. We missed the rest of the good pool weather, but I was happy enough sitting on my balcony with a White Claw or a tumbler of bourbon.

On the rocks. It was a sudden inspiration one Saturday afternoon, and I found that I liked it.

When she finally agreed to meet me, I suggested Shain Park of all places. We picked up some shawarma from the Mediterranean place and walked over to the park, found a bench, and sat in the autumn sun. Summer had taken its toll on the perfect grass, turning patches brown. From where we were sitting, we could see the Freedom Sculpture, though we were looking at the figures' backs.

I told her why I did it. I said I was living by the Ethos. I gave her every reason I could think of why it was time to stop: her health, the heat, the fact that she was guzzling ibuprofen like candy. And, of course, there was a threat on her life.

She was wearing a brace on her hand and wrist. Only the tips of her fingers reached out through the brace, making it hard to handle her shawarma. "It was my decision," she said. "And you stole that from me."

"I guess, even when I'm trying to be good, I mess things up," I said.

She gave me a half smile. "Maybe you did the right thing—I don't know. But you did it the wrong way."

I looked down at the cement. I knew what she was saying. She was talking about the standing board, and she was talking about our night together, too. I should have talked with her. And I shouldn't have made my move when we were drunk.

She stood up. She was short, so she barely had to lean over to kiss me on the cheek. Then she whispered in my ear: "I believe in you." She said goodbye, and I guess she meant it, because I haven't really seen her since. A couple of times in passing, but we don't hang out anymore. No more White Claws at the pool. I guess her parents think I'm great, but I think they suck, so it doesn't mean a whole lot.

It's been a couple of years now, but someone will still occasionally ask me about Kyleigh and World Upside Down. They might have heard that I was friends with Kyleigh, and they want to know what I think about it. And I suppose, in one sense, they're asking whether Kyleigh was legit—whether she was really trying to make a difference or just stumping for attention. But there's another aspect to the question— whether it made a lick of difference. And that the part's harder to answer.

On the one hand, I don't think much more of humanity than I did. Most people spend their lives hiding from themselves. People are cowards, they really are. But every once in a while, I'll be sitting on my little balcony, or I'll be out on the lake in Vicksburg, and I'll have a vision of Kyleigh at her standing board. Not just a memory, but a vision, if you know what I mean—like it's something I'm *supposed* to see. I know it sounds weird, but it's the truth, as far as I can tell it. So yeah, I still think about Kyleigh and her standing board, and I guess that answers the question right there. Did it matter? Yeah. Sure, it did. At least for me.

I still act like an ass sometimes, don't get me wrong. I'm not a fundamentally different person. But I want to be. And that's how people change, right? They start wanting something different. Longing for something different. That's some powerful shit right there. It's uncomfortable as hell, but I hope it never goes away.

Crime and Punishment

On the internet, Sarah learned how to make a pick set from a couple of old nail files. Her ex-husband, Mark, took most of his tools when he moved out, but he'd left the massive workbench on the side of the garage where he used to park his BMW. He also left some of the tools he presumably didn't need: a hammer, set of screw drivers, adjustable wrench, and a pair of pliers.

Making the pick set only took a few minutes. Learning to pick a lock wasn't that difficult either, even with a pair of jerry-rigged nail files. She practiced for an hour, working on both of her own doors. Then she took a break for lunch and drove her SUV two blocks to the deli for lunch.

This was what it was like as a single adult. She went out to dinner with friends or ordered from the Thai place she and Mark had frequented for years. For lunch, she paid someone else to make her a sandwich. It was a sad state of affairs, but she never felt like getting groceries. She did occasionally run to the natural food market to load up on granola bars, cereal, yogurt, microwave burritos, and wine.

It was late for lunch, and the deli was nearly empty. She took a seat at a corner booth, hovering over her Caesar chicken wrap and her phone, texting with Gretchen from work. Gretchen had been her mainstay, the one she'd turned to when things with Mark became difficult.

It was Mark who'd finally pronounced them incompatible. Their chemistry had been powerful from the start. In the beginning, they stayed up all night together, as if they were supercharged.

They had taken a weekend trip to northern Michigan. They skied for a day and a half and, exhausted, spent the second afternoon in the indoor water park. There was a river that circled the park, and it looked appealing at first, sitting in a tube and floating, soaking in the humid air. But after two trips around the lazy river, they grew bored and decided to try the water slides. "No lazy river for us," they said. It became a saying in their relationship. No lazy river. Anything but boredom.

After several months of bliss, though, they started fighting. They argued about money. Both were jealous. The sex was great, but the pattern of disintegration and recovery was exhausting.

During the lunch rush, the restaurant would have been filled with the sounds of customers: the murmuring din, the click and gush of the fountain machine. Occasionally, a staff member called out an order. Now, though, in the quiet of the early afternoon, she couldn't help but overhear the conversation between two employees, a teenage boy and girl. They were talking about a co-worker, named Jay, who hadn't shown up for work. She heard about Jay's problems, which included a misspelled tattoo, a sister who'd kicked him out, and, above all else, his girlfriend. *She* was possessive. *She* didn't let him out of her sight. *She* kept him from graduating high school, from having other friends, from making it to work.

Sarah tried ignoring them, but it proved impossible, and her irritation grew as she ate her lunch. She chewed hard, wished she'd brought her earbuds. Finally, she couldn't tolerate it any longer. She crumpled the wax paper in her fist and walked to the counter.

"Yes," the girl said. She was wearing short shorts, and from the front it looked like she was naked beneath her apron.

"Do you have parents?" Sarah asked, making eye contact with both teens.

"Uh, yeah," the boy answered.

"Interesting," she said. "Because it doesn't seem like anyone has taught you anything about life."

They were shocked. They thought she was going to ask for

extra napkins or a drink. "When someone misses work," she continued, "whose fault is it?"

The boy stared, dumbfounded. The girl's eyes dropped to her razor burned thighs and knobby knees.

"It's their own damn fault," Sarah said, raising her eyebrows to punctuate her point. She threw away her wrapper and stalked away. She flung open the door. It swung wide, hesitated, then came shuddering closed behind her.

She had hours to kill, but even though she could use the sleep, she couldn't imagine napping. Mark would be in bed by midnight, probably earlier, but she wasn't going to chance it. The plan was to leave at one-thirty, which would get her to his new house by two in the morning. He was a solid sleeper. By then, he'd be comatose.

Mark had stayed at the Residence Inn for six months. In the beginning, they were still in touch, discussing the terms of their divorce. Sometimes, they were even nice to one another. When she figured out he was watching her on the home security cameras, that was the end of her civility. She stopped talking. They were down to text messages and lawyers.

She knew he'd moved out of the extended-stay, because he came to pick up furniture: a futon they kept in the basement, a back-up coffee table from the garage, a set of Windsor chairs stacked in the attic. She spent that day with Gretchen, running errands and checking out a new brewery. When she got home that night, everything in the house was the same, except he had left his dirty footprints all over the floors. In the tiled kitchen, she could even see the tread. It was a perfect metaphor for their relationship. From one vantage point, she was unchanged. Unmoved. Also she was trampled.

She learned about his new place (an old farmhouse out in Mason, across from the Maplewoods Farm Stand) from a mutual friend. Mark had always wanted a tractor and an old house with a covered porch. Now, with his ex out of the picture, he could finally move out to the country and spend his weekends moving piles of dirt around, building fencing he didn't need, and planting fruit trees he would never prune or spray—that would never give him anything but a bunch of worm-eaten apples.

In the middle of the night, she left home, took the highway, then a paved county road, and then a dirt road that seemed okay at first, but eventually turned into a washboard. Her vehicle shook, tires grinding over the ribbed surface. In back, the gasoline sloshed in its red container. She leaned over her steering wheel, scanning the road as she drove. She still hit two big potholes, each time with a bang.

At the farm stand, she killed her lights and coasted to a stop. When she'd driven here during the day, scoping it out, it had felt inhabited. These were rural homes and small family farms on narrow fields littered with barns, sheds, and hoop houses. In the dark, though, it felt terribly wild. She shivered. She slid her arms into the sleeves of her jacket and checked her pockets. A gust of wind rushed through the open fields, bending a stand of pines, riffling her sleeves.

By moonlight, she walked along the edge of the road, following the shadows of electrical wires overhead, sag and rejoinder, sag and rejoinder. Occasionally, she passed beneath the arm of a large tree, its long shadow reaching across the road. She shifted the gas can from one hand to the other, her body warming with exertion.

Where the driveway met the road, there was a lone street-light. She heard the bird-chirp of bats and saw them swooping through the spray of light. Despite her fear, she continued, nearly dragging the can of gasoline, until she reached the driveway and the house appeared. It was probably unnecessary, but she stalked through long grass away from the streetlight, thankful the wind covered the sound of her movements. She made a mental note to check later for ticks and angled toward the garage, where Mark housed his beloved BMW diesel.

Their biggest fight happened the day Mark brought the car home. She knew he'd been looking online sporadically for months but she didn't know he had found the model he was looking for, less than an hour away, at a dealership in Ionia. A friend gave him a ride, and he drove the Beemer home, right up the driveway. Smiling.

At first, she didn't say anything. She didn't have to. He knew she'd be mad. He knew she'd say no, which is why he didn't ask. An hour later, he was washing his hands at the sink when she cornered him. "I can't believe you would buy a car without even talking to me about it."

"It's my money." He didn't turn around to speak to her.

It was a line they circled back to for the rest of their marriage. She could justify any purchase with the expression: *it's my money*, offered up with a shrug. In reality, they had a joint bank account and everything was mixed together. Assets. Expenses. It certainly didn't help with the divorce.

The house was dark, and she could only see a few steps ahead, relying on the dim light of stars, faint under a haze of clouds. The moon seemed to have disappeared. Exhausted, she set the gas can next to the side garage door. It was a good thing she was fit. She was overly concerned with her appearance; she could admit that. But it kept her in shape.

As she worked on the lock, she heard something scratching in a woodpile next to the door. She was terrified of mice, and it was impossible to pick the lock while her heart jumped inside her chest. She backed away from the door and turned on her phone's flashlight. The creature was hidden, but she knew it was there, scurrying and nibbling. For a moment, she felt like she couldn't breathe. The possibility she was having a heart attack passed through her mind. What a way to die—on the ground outside her ex-husband's garage next to a can of gasoline.

Eventually, she caught her breath and slowed her heart rate. She listened for the mouse, but the sound was gone, and again she approached the door. She reached out her hand, and, out of habit, turned the knob. It was unlocked.

As she entered the garage, her heart started racing again, beating so hard it almost hurt. Again, she paused, bent over, took a moment to catch her breath. With the phone light, she traced the circumference of the garage. In one corner were garden tools: a hard rake and a leaf rake leaning against the wall, hand tools suspended from hooks. In another corner, his skis and poles. Next to the door to the house, a pile of boxes that would be there forever. And there, right in the middle of it all: the BMW. Waiting for her. The car was blue, but under the flashlight's glare, it looked silver. The still-perfect paint job sprayed light up at the ceiling.

She headed for the driver's side, still lugging the gas can, which only seemed to be getting heavier. Her jacket swished as she moved, and the heavy container banged against her leg. She paused and listened to the wind throw itself against the garage.

As she took her next step, there was a loud high-pitched noise. She froze, trying to ignore the pain in her shoulder, the gas can's weight stretching her ligaments. When she was able to think, she realized the sound came from outside, most likely an owl and its prey. Her heart had just about jumped out of her throat.

What she hadn't considered: the BMW's gas tank cover was locked. It could only be opened with a lever by the driver's seat inside the car, and if she tried opening the door, she might trigger the alarm.

Leaving the gas can next to the car, she snuck over to the door that led into the house. It, too, was unlocked. But when she tried to ease the door open, it caught, stuck in the jam. She looked at the door, trying to decide what to do next, whether to push on the stuck door and risk the noise.

There were moments when Sarah wondered whether she was sane. There was just so much anger, hurt, and disappointment. Sometimes it consumed her. On a drive home from getting take-out or running an errand, she would start thinking about Mark and the surveillance cameras. She would start working on a letter to him, composing it in her mind, and she would miss her exit, not even realizing until she was halfway to Detroit.

There were days, too, when she got almost nothing done at work, she was so distracted thinking about what she wanted to say to him—or dreaming up ways she could hurt him. Finally, she settled on the car. Whenever she thought she was taking it too far, she would think about Gretchen when she told her what Mark had done. Gretchen had flipped out. "Oh my God, oh my God," she'd said. No, this was an equal and opposite reaction.

She knew he'd mounted security cameras in their house right after he bought the BMW. He installed the software on his computer, and she never paid much attention. It was several months after he moved out before she realized he was using the cameras to spy on her. She'd been walking across the kitchen, moving through light, streaming in through the window over the sink. It was one of those bright days in early spring, and the flecks of mica in the granite countertops were shimmering, and the whole world seemed to slow down. It was a moment of hyper-awareness: she saw the security camera mounted above a door frame and realized it was still on.

She disconnected the cameras in the kitchen and the garage—the ones she knew about—and then confronted him over the phone, though she now wished she'd been able to see his face when he tried to play it off.

"I want our house to be secure," he'd said.

"You aren't living here," she said.

He rambled about the fact that it was still his house, his biggest financial asset.

She cut him off. "You're watching me," she said. "Admit it."

"That's not what this is about."

"You want to know if I'm seeing someone else."

He refused to come clean.

She found the other camera in a fit of cleaning. It was a warm spell at the end of winter, and she'd decided to wash the bedroom windows inside and out, which led to wiping down the window trim, which led to taking everything off the built-in bookshelves, even the highest shelf, which she never touched. And there it was: a little camera tucked in the shadow of a large volume of European history, a book from college. He'd been watching her dress and undress. He may have even seen her masturbate. After the separation, Gretchen had suggested porn, and she had found some new things she didn't know she liked.

"Fuck," she screamed. She threw the camera to the ground, but it just slid across the floor. She retrieved it, sliding on the kitchen tile as she ran to the garage. She found a hammer, put it on the concrete floor, and smashed the thing to bits.

She decided to risk it. She pushed against the door, and it popped open with just a squeak. She paused, trying to manage her breathing. When she didn't hear anything, she eased her way into the house. Of course, the kitchen was a mess. Stacks of paper plates and cups on the counter, still in their packaging. Silverware piled in the sink. He would let the dishes and the laundry go until he didn't have a clean dish or a piece of clothing left to wear. One thing she would never miss was picking up after him.

She looked for his keys but didn't see them. The house was quiet, except for the heater humming in the basement. To be sure he was sleeping, she tiptoed down the hallway and peered up the stairs. Yes, she heard Mark snoring like a drone—she didn't miss that either.

She decided to forget the car and look for another act of sabotage. She'd loved the idea of ruining his diesel-powered car with a few gallons of unleaded gasoline, him speeding off to work in the morning completely unaware that he was destroying the engine. But now that she was here, she realized she couldn't go through with it. The car was too expensive. It was too much.

She changed the clock on his oven, the only clock she could find, turning it back ten minutes. What else? She was less and less concerned about being caught. He was asleep and didn't own a gun. What was the worst that could happen?

His computer was on the coffee table. She tried a few of the passwords she knew he used. None worked. She tried the name of his new road. No. For kicks, she tried the date of their wedding anniversary, and voila, she was in.

Hovering over his computer in the middle of the night, none of it felt real. She could hear his snoring, and, from a distance, it sounded peaceful. She could picture his sleeping face: eyes closed, lips parted. His vulnerability caused her anger to retreat. It was still there, but it was harder to access.

If she could get into his bank accounts, that would be something. But when it came to his banking, he wasn't going to dick around with an old password or an anniversary date. She thought about going into his Facebook and posting a confession in his voice. "I am writing this message because I want to apologize to my ex-wife, Sarah, and I believe it's important to make this a public statement." The letter would spell out his crimes: How he bought the BMW without consulting her, flirted with other women in front of her, and how he spied on her with the home security system, because he was jealous and wanted to know if she was seeing someone. And also because he was a pervert. Thinking through the contents of the apology helped to rekindle the anger that brought her here. But she didn't write the letter, because she knew she wouldn't post it. What she wanted was for him to feel what she felt when she discovered the cameras.

On a strip of cardboard from one of Mark's moving boxes, using a sharpie from the kitchen counter, she wrote: "I'm Watching You," in block letters, took a photo, and made the picture his desktop background. Then she took a photo of her hand, giving him the middle finger, and set the image as his screen saver, ready to pop up after two minutes. She thought about setting the away message on his email to something embarrassing, then decided against it. But she did order a Shinola watch she had been eyeing, using his Amazon account and scheduled it for delivery to her house. It was five hundred dollars, enough to seem outrageous, though he could afford it. She waited for the confirmation email to come in and deleted it. He would find out eventually. Even when he did, he wouldn't freak. One nice thing about Mark: he wasn't cheap.

The watch gave her a dose of satisfaction. She had accomplished something, not as dramatic as she'd intended, but for a moment she basked in the glow of the computer light. She stretched her back, arching like a cat. She wanted to get out of the drafty old farmhouse. She was cold.

Moving through the house, she again felt anxious about waking him. Avoiding furniture and half-empty boxes, she made it back to the garage door, twisted the knob and pulled. It squeaked. She hesitated, swung the damn thing open. It bellowed the whole way like a crying child.

She heard Mark shift upstairs. His bed groan, then his feet on the floor. There was only one thing to do. She slipped into the garage, grabbed the gas can, and hauled ass. Trying to run with the gas can was like doing a three-legged race with an unwilling partner. Gasoline sloshed and leaked out through the air valve she'd forgotten to close tight.

She lumbered down the driveway, switching the gas can from one side to the other. She tried holding it in front of her with both hands, but her knees kept banging the plastic can, now slicked with stinking gasoline. Still, she was getting away, if she could just make it to the road.

The outdoor lights burst on. Knowing Mark would step outside any moment, she cut for the road. The long grass didn't offer much cover, but there were trees about thirty feet away, and shadow beneath the tree line.

She didn't make it. Stepping off the driveway, her right foot landed in a hole. The gas can in her right hand, her step landed with force, and she fell. Her ankle screamed with pain and she dropped the can.

Mark was coming down the driveway. She wanted to at least hide the gas can, but the trees were still twenty feet away, and she knew she couldn't stand. She didn't even think she could crawl. Instead, she lay on her back, panting. "God," she moaned, "I am such an idiot." She touched her ankle, and it was already swollen. She would be lucky if it wasn't broken. "Fuck, fuck, fuck."

"Brava, Brava," Mark applauded, as he reached the scene. "Umm…what in the holy fuck is going on?"

He was wearing his bathrobe with no shirt, and she could see his clavicle, his bare ankles. His hair was tousled in a way she always liked. It was thick, and dark, and looked good, even by accident. Especially by accident.

"What does it look like?" she responded.

"It looks like you're lying in my driveway, injured, next to a can of gasoline?" He righted the can of gasoline.

"I stepped in a hole," she said. "It's freezing, and my ankle is killing me. Will you please help me?"

"Gladly," he said. He had a smirk on his face. She always hated that. He was so fucking smug.

He helped her to her feet, and they moved toward the house. She couldn't put any weight on her ankle. Not an ounce. He was six inches taller than she, so he hunched over, her arm looped over his shoulders. Their steps were linked.

The front porch light buzzed, its glass coated with decades worth of dust, grime, and dead bugs. The steps were tricky. He practically hauled her up to the stoop.

She wanted to sit and started to disentangle herself. But he stopped her.

"Just a little further," he said.

He pushed the door open, and she hopped to the couch and fell into it. While she caught her breath, Mark fetched a bucket of ice water.

"This is going to be cold," he said.

"Really?"

"I'm trying to be nice," he said.

He was right. She was in no position to be snarky. "Sorry," she said.

She tried rolling up her pants, but they were too tight, and she didn't want to get them wet. For a moment, she hesitated, but what was the difference? So she unbuttoned her jeans and started squirming out of them. Mark handed her a blanket so she could cover herself.

Taking a deep breath, she plunged her foot into the ice water. It was so cold it hurt. But she held it there and waited for the foot to go numb. Eventually, the pain eased.

Mark made coffee and sat across from her. It was good. He always made good coffee—that was another thing she missed.

He asked her about the gas can.

She looked at the old floorboards. "I was going to put gasoline in the BMW." She bit her lip. It was strange, talking with Mark about it. She had gone over all of this with Gretchen but never imagined holding a dispassionate conversation with her ex-husband regarding his crime and punishment. She said it was what he deserved, even if, in the end, she had decided not to follow through. "It's too expensive," she said. "And kind of pointless."

He nodded. He was willing to play along. "The BMW is out of bounds," he said.

"Oh, really," she countered. "So now we're deciding what's out of bounds."

He smiled. "Okay, that's fair."

She was trying to decide what she wanted from this moment. Did she want him to suffer? Was she looking for an apology? Did she want to see him grovel? To beg her to come back? Did she want sex?

"I don't know," she said. "I guess I'm just still mad about the BMW. You should have talked with me about it. I'm not unreasonable."

"You're right." He crossed his legs. He looked ridiculous in his robe.

"I like those words," she said. She was about to add something glib but pulled back. Her anger was retreating, like the swelling in her ankle. What she wanted, she now realized, wasn't to cause him pain. Rather, she wanted hers acknowledged.

"I was so mad about the cameras," she said. "I *am* so mad." She looked down at her ankle, at the ice floating in the freezing water. "Knowing that you were watching me."

"The thing is…" He paused. He recrossed his legs, switching sides. "I'm sorry."

It was the thing she had wanted more than anything else, and now she didn't know what to say. She had heard how athletes who win a medal at the Olympics are often confused afterward. They train for years, and they get the thing they wanted, and then have no idea what to do next. She felt that uncertainty now. She was relieved. Grateful. Lost.

Dawn was breaking. New light pressed into the house, making everything glow. Now she could see all the boxes, frames leaning against the wall, drop cloths covering furniture where he was preparing to paint. The mess of moving.

"Life is so fucking crazy," she said. She started the day learning how to pick a lock, ended the day by sneaking into her ex-husband's house where she'd done some party tricks on his computer, sprained her ankle and got caught with a can of gasoline she'd hauled all over the place and never used. Now they were sitting together, actually talking.

"No lazy river for us," he said.

"No," she agreed. "No lazy river."

Mark had a pair of crutches, and he made them shorter for her. He went to fetch her car, and that left her alone again. She took her foot out of the ice water, patted it dry. It was a perfect morning. The farmhouse knew exactly how to take the light. It rushed through the windows, made rectangles on the floors. The house knew exactly where it belonged; it was incredibly certain. Even now, birds were collecting straw, making homes in the eaves. She could never live in a place like this.

Crashums

"COME ON, DAD, I'M PLAYING CRASHUMS," Stanley called from the living room. Stanley was four. Crashums was a game we made up where we sent one of Stanley's toy cars down a track and into another one with a crash.

I was standing in the kitchen with my then-wife, Mariah. She was still in her pajamas, a getup I called her prison stripes. It was white with blue pinstripes. She used to argue with me saying that prison clothes had horizontal stripes, and that right there is one of the differences between us: she can't take a joke. From the living room, I heard a car go flying down the track and slam into its victim. Zip, crack.

Mariah's thick hair was piled on top of her head and held together with these fat hairpins that looked like chopsticks, and she was leaning forward to take a sip of coffee.

"Tate seems to be handling things all right," I said. Tate, our ten-year-old, was upstairs. He often disappeared with a book, sometimes for hours. I knew Mariah disagreed, but it seemed to me that Tate, as mature as he was, could handle the situation. Possibly he could manage things better than his parents.

Tate had confronted his mother weeks before, and he knew the basic run-down. Apparently, he said to Mariah: "Are you and Dad getting a divorce?" Mariah tried playing dumb, but he kept at it until she admitted we were separating. Tate had a way of seeing through you even if you put up a good front.

Mariah rinsed her coffee mug in the sink and stared blankly out the window. I walked into the living room and stood behind Stanley. He had run a stretch of orange track from the couch down to the floor using a cushion to hold the top of the track in place. It was a nice effort for a four year old except the track kept slipping out from under the cushion.

Stanley sniffed. His nose was dripping.

I found a roll of clear packing tape and taped the track to the couch, fitting the tape into the contours of the plastic. Then I ran a Mustang GT into a fire truck. Zip, crack. The fire truck barely budged.

When I'd entered the house that morning, Mariah met me in the breezeway and told me that she had taken the boys to a rescue shelter the day before, but that they had come home without a dog. She decided at the last moment that she couldn't do it—she didn't want anything else to take care of. To make it up to the boys, she took them out for ice cream, and that was enough for Stanley, but Tate was still upset. I don't blame him. That was the sort of thing that drove me crazy about her.

"Dad," Stanley said, "it's not working." His nose was completely clogged, and his consonants sounded gooey like he was eating Elmers, and the glue was stuck in his throat. He seemed to always have a cold.

The packing tape had come unstuck, and the track had fallen to the floor. I picked it up and started removing the tape while Stanley pushed his cars around on the hardwood.

"Be right back, sport," I said and went to the basement looking for a roll of duck tape. But when I returned with the roll dangling around my wrist, I decided not to use the heavy tape on the new microfiber couch. I started trying to convince Stanley that we should move our set-up to the window, but he shouted, "I want it this way," and threw himself on the floor, face first, legs flailing as I started carrying the track across the room.

Until this moment, I had been able to hold it together. I'd survived Mariah's whole routine about the shelter and the fact that she'd barely said a word to me all morning. My mother had given me a pretty good speech about keeping things civil, and I was doing my best. I'll admit, Stanley's little tantrum put me over the edge, and I got on his case pretty good: "For crying out loud, Stanley," I said. "Don't be such a baby—I'm just moving the track."

It was just like Mariah to appear right in the middle of a difficult moment, hovering, hands on her hips, still in those ridiculous pajamas, and judging me the way she always did.

"This is exactly the problem," I said to her. "You won't ever just give me a break."

Mariah turned and walked back into the kitchen, and I was left with Stanley, who was sobbing and making a puddle of tears and snot on the floor.

"Come on, bud," I said. "I like your track, but it isn't working."

He looked up. "I want it this way," he said again. It sounded like, "dis bay," his nose was so full of snot.

It was at this moment that Tate decided to appear, stepping over Stanley and flopping onto the couch.

"What's for breakfast?" Tate asked.

"The rest of us had breakfast an hour ago, but you can make yourself an egg."

He swooned, falling backward like he was suffering from heat stroke.

"I don't like eggs," he said.

"That's news to me."

"Well," he argued, "things change."

I looked down. The oak floor was scuffed and scratched from its years of sacrifice. "Make yourself a piece of toast," I said.

"Fine," he said, but he didn't move. He just lay on his back, staring up at the ceiling, as if awaiting some heavenly revelation. At a loss, I again started for the window, hoping Stanley would now go along with the change. But he started up again.

"Stanley. For shit's sake," I said.

That was enough to bring Mariah back from the kitchen. "If you can't get your act together..." She stopped, but I knew exactly how she intended to finish that sentence. She was threatening to throw me out of my own damn house.

It's strange how rage works. On the one hand, when it comes over you, it takes over completely like a second brain overruling the first. But on the other hand, even while you're being carried away, there is a line of rational thought that continues, evaluating everything as it is happening. And so, even as I was doing it, I remember thinking that it was a childish thing to do, even as I whacked that plastic track hard against the wall, the track swinging like a rope, cracking against the wall like a whip snapping at its apex, breaking the air. I swung it a second time and a third, but the track got twisted, landed awkwardly, and the sound didn't come. A stab of pain grabbed my shoulder and hot tears started burning my eyes.

"I can't do anything," I yelled.

Stanley and Tate were both frozen. Mariah stood there watching me, but instead of looking angry, now she looked frightened. She looked like the top of the house had blown off, and we were standing together in the open air—the four walls of our suburban home without a ceiling or a roof, and rain pouring down on our unprotected life. And it's the strangest thing, but I remember at that very moment thinking about what it sounds like when a flock of geese passes overhead, their cries dissipating as they fade into the distance.

For a moment, I stood there, looking at the wall where I had struck it as hard as I could but without leaving a mark, and then I walked out onto the back porch. It was a three-season porch, and we'd forever been talking about turning it into a four-season: adding insulation and replacing the windows, though we'd never done anything about it. I stood right outside the door, just on the other side of the living room, looking at the sad November grass and rubbing my bare arms against the cold.

When I came back inside, I found Stanley where I'd left him, playing with his cars. Tate was at the kitchen island, eating toast and scrambled eggs of all things. I picked Stanley up and whispered, "I'm sorry, buddy. I'm so sorry," into his ear, and he tucked his head into my shoulder. Mariah was standing behind Tate, and she put her hands on his back, and I carried Stanley over to the island, so that, in a way we were all connected, even if part of that link was a granite countertop.

Tate said, "I'm still mad about the dog," and we all laughed, Stanley laughing the hardest, though he didn't have any idea what the joke was about.

"Hey Stan," I said. "Let's play Crashums outside in the driveway." I knew he'd like the idea.

"Yeah," he said, wiping his nose on his arm.

I took the packing tape and the track, and Stanley brought the cars. I taped the track to a drain-spout, and we sent the cars flying down the blacktop. Eventually, Tate followed us outside. His hair was pin-straight, and it kept falling over his eyes.

He asked for the GT. It was our favorite, and I pulled it out of my pocket.

"How far do you think she'll go?" I asked. But he had that faraway look he gets sometimes, and it was like he didn't hear me.

"Dad," he said. "I'm worried that everything is going to change."

I saw Mariah in the window peeking around the curtain, and I wondered what she would say. I'll give credit where credit's due. She always seemed to know what to say even when the shit was all caving in.

"Sometimes it feels that way," I said. "But it isn't really true. Some things always stay the same."

Tate wore glasses, and he did this thing where he touched the hook of his glasses, where it wrapped around his ear, and then held his earlobe between his fingers. He was holding onto his earlobe while we talked.

"Like what?" he asked.

"Mom and I will always love you," I said. "And Stan the Man here will always have a runny nose."

"That's true," he said. "What else?" Stanley sent a car flying down the track out of control, flipping over itself. He came over and sat in my lap, and I wiped his nose with my shirt.

"What else?" I repeated. I patted Stan on the head and felt his thick hair and remembered how he had nothing but peach fuzz for the first year of his life.

"You," I said. "You will always be you, the only Tate in the world."

He made a face at me like, "What the hell, Dad? That's not an answer."

Just then Mariah came out the front door and stood beside us. "What are you guys doing?" she asked.

"Unfolding the mysteries of the universe," I said.

"Let me know if you have any luck with that."

"We're trying," Tate said. "We're doing our best."

"That we are," I said.

"Sounds like quite a conversation."

Then I had a thought that made sense to me: this whole experience was like an earthquake shaking our life, and all we could really do is wait it out, hoping that there's something left when it's done. I looked up at Mariah. Loose strands of her hair were dancing in a breeze. She had another cup of coffee and was sipping it the way she does with her head bent over her mug.

I watched her and tried to think of something to say, but it was all so complicated. How do you find words when every feeling inside you is in competition with something else, when every ounce of anger is matched with an equivalent measure of regret? Maybe it's impossible to make sense of something like that until it's past and you have the luxury of looking back.

It was just as those thoughts were running through my mind when I noticed Tate. He was standing next to Mariah, his hands latched to her waist, and it looked as if she was holding him up. And I thought, *Yes, that's it, Tate. Keep holding on.*

Auras

He first saw it at the grocery store. He had just turned down the pasta aisle, gliding past the boxes of mac and cheese. This was early in the outbreak. In the past month, schools were closed, restaurants converted into takeout and delivery hubs. People were uncertain, moving like electrons through the store repelled by a shared negative charge.

What he saw was an orange glow, coming from the frame of a metal shelf, a three-inch oval, undefined at its edges, pulsing. He inched toward it, altered his line of sight. In the fluorescent light, it could almost have been a reflection. And when he left the store, that's what he told himself. A bad bulb. A trick of light. Within a couple of hours, he put it out of his mind. Until it happened again.

Markus, originally from a suburb of Frankfurt called Bornheim, was the Midwest sales rep for a German company that built coffee and espresso machines. Just a week ago, the sales team had made jokes on their conference call about the necessity of coffee. *Man can't live on bread alone; he needs his cup of joe! You think COVID's bad, try caffeine withdrawal!* But he knew his job was in jeopardy. This wasn't some fabled Italian espresso maker; it was *Kaffeeblitz*, a boring but solid product made by conscientious Germans. For the past ten years, they had been slowly carving out market share in the U.S., but in the midst of a crisis, who was running out to buy an above-average coffee machine? Personally, he was using a French press and had been since his divorce.

He didn't know when he would get to see his six-year-old daughter, Agnes. His ex, Mary, kept putting him off. When he asked how she was managing work and errands with Agnes home all day, she was evasive.

"I make it work," she said.

"What about me? When do I get to see my daughter?"

"Markus, you're a traveling salesman, *Traveling!* Who knows what you've been exposed to?" He could have argued. He hadn't traveled in weeks. He hadn't seen a soul. But it wasn't worth it.

The only consistent thing in his life was his dog, Otto, a Jack Russel Terrier, young and energetic. When a visitor came knocking, he leaped at the door, and when the guest entered the house, tried to climb them. With all that energy, he required two walks per day.

The weather was erratic in March, but this day was pleasant, fifty degrees and sunny. Markus wore a vest, and a hat, and was sweating as Otto dragged him along. In many respects, America had fulfilled his stereotype as a social wild west. He saw it when he picked up his daughter from elementary school and many of the parents refused to follow the school guidelines, leaving their engines running as they waited in their cars, instead of walking to retrieve their children. When the virus first appeared, people stockpiled goods, ignoring the signs at the grocery store. Limit one per customer meant nothing to these rugged individualists.

Behavior did start improving as the pandemic took hold. Mostly, this meant staying home. The main emphasis of health experts was distancing. Masks were reserved for doctors and nurses. People were encouraged to go to a park for exercise, to stay healthy and keep up morale.

As he walked, he listened to music. His playlist was dominated by contemporary folk, singer-songwriters, and Americana: The Ballroom Thieves, Sharon Van Etten, Caitlin Canty. He was generally thrifty, but he'd finally talked himself into an expensive pair of earbuds.

He noticed the orange glow when he crossed the street to a small city park. It was on the arm of a park bench, several blotches of vivid orange, just like the one he'd seen in the grocery store. In the daylight, the phenomenon was unmistakable. There was a man sitting on the bench. He was an older man with a gray beard tucked inside a plaid scarf. Less than a meter away from a glowing orange phenomenon, he seemed completely unaware.

Markus turned off his music. Because he, like everyone else, had COVID constantly on his mind, his very next thought was that he was seeing the virus itself. It seemed impossible, but so did the whole scenario: millions of people home from work, millions filing for unemployment, factories closed, hospitals flooded with patients. So why not?

He jogged home, tugging on Otto's leash, every time his dog wanted to stop to pee and sniff. Grabbing a box of sanitizing wipes, he returned to the park.

The bearded man was still there. Markus shortened Otto's leash and walked toward the bench, the arm glowing with what he now recognized as three distinct spots.

"Nice day," he said to the man.

"It is," the man agreed. "Spring," he added, in explanation.

The man pivoted his body toward the orange spots as they talked, unaware or unconcerned with their presence.

"Do you see that?" Markus asked.

"See what?"

"Oh nothing," he said.

Markus came alongside the bench. With a gloved hand, he took a sanitizing wipe and slid it along the bench's arm.

For a moment, nothing happened. He had been confident that the wipe would work, that it would kill the virus and make the spot disappear. But there it was, still active, still burning. He turned and looked over the park. Much of the grass was trodden and flattened to the earth. Tree branches showed no buds. When he looked again at the bench, he saw that the glow was fading; the spots were melting away, turning translucent, until he could again see the dark green color of the fake wood. The wipe worked; it just took a few seconds to do so.

At home, he removed the gloves, turning them inside-out. He washed his hands for a full minute, soaping them twice. Then he drove to Mary's house in his mid-sized Ford sedan. He rolled slowly past on the far side of the road. There was no sign of the virus anywhere on the front of the house. The door handle was clean. Mailbox, too. Agnes's bike was sitting in front of an open garage door, and it too, was free of the virus.

He continued to the grocery store where he'd first seen the glow. Afraid, he sat in the car, letting it idle. He wanted to go home, but he also wanted to see the virus again. A song on the radio ended, and he shut off the car, pocketed the keys. He started in the bakery. Nothing. Past the dairy case. Nothing.

He turned down the pasta aisle and there it was—that spot, still glowing, though it seemed to have faded. He looked at the display of food, pretending to shop, while he waited for the aisle to clear. Then he killed it with a disinfectant wipe. A search of the store revealed several more sites, mostly on the aluminum shelves and on the stainless-steel case of one of the conveyor belts at checkout.

He visited two more grocery stores, three playgrounds, and a half-dozen gas stations. He was listening to a bluegrass mix: Nickel Creek, Della Mae, Allison Krauss and Union Station. The twang of the banjo, the knee-slap drive of the music lent an urgency to his mission, although he kept striking out. It was only when he was about to give up when he discovered the infected gas station. He first saw the glow on a pump handle. Inside, he found several more spots: on a drink cooler and on the edge of the checkout counter, a bit of virus that escaped when staff wiped down the surface. Afterward, he peeled off another pair of gloves and pumped a large dose of sanitizer into his hands. He reminded himself that he was young and healthy; he didn't have any reason to be afraid.

The next day was more of the same. Hunting for virus, only he mellowed back to folk. Tall Heights and the Wailin' Jennys: harmony and strings, a wash of sound. He drove past Mary's again.

Otto was bouncing off the walls when he got home, and he took him for a walk, even though it was cold and drizzling. Later, he had a dissatisfying video chat with Agnes. Six year olds are terrible on the phone and even worse on a video call. She spent the entire time looking at herself and making faces. He considered talking to Mary again, pushing for a visit, but stopped himself. With Mary, there was a line; he knew from experience.

Once, when they were still married, they had a fight, and Mary didn't speak to him for three entire days. She didn't yell. She didn't slam doors or cupboards. She just stopped talking, like a spigot frozen shut.

He apologized. He made a nice dinner. He tried egging her into another fight. Nothing worked. Then, on the evening of the third day, she answered a question. Slowly, the spigot opened.

After ending his chat with Agnes, he called his sister in California. She had moved to the States twenty years before, when their parents were still alive.

"Wie geht's, Caroline?"

"Oh, you know," she said. "Langweilig. We wait, we watch the news."

"Ja," he said, leaning forward and tapping his finger on the coffee table.

California was one of the first states to go into lockdown mode, and so far, it seemed to be working. Michigan had taken many of the same precautions, but the virus was spreading in Detroit. In the news, they were calling it the next hotspot.

"Mary won't let me see Agnes," he said. "Because of my travel."

Caroline sided with Mary. She said it was sensible, considering her asthma.

"Natürlich," he said. Soon after, he ended the conversation.

On Facebook the next morning, he learned that a friend tested positive. "Temperature is 103," the post said. "Everybody stay home!"

Dave was in his fifties, a pipefitter, overweight and diabetic. They met through trivia night at a local brewery, the same brewery where Markus occasionally played his folky originals with a mix of pop covers to keep the audience's attention. Dave often made jokes about his weight, his disdain for exercise. None of that seemed funny now.

When it was dark, he drove to Dave's and parked around the corner. He found a spot on the porch railing and cleaned it, watching the orange glow fade into nothing. Otherwise, there was no sign of the virus, just a dark house, set back further than its neighbors, as if retreating from the streetlights.

He considered heading home, but he felt an impulse to keep looking. He circled the house, a small ranch, lifting his feet as he walked over the dew-soaked grass. He thought he heard a noise, high-pitched and distant, but he wasn't sure. It was like a subconscious thought; he knew it was there, but it was impossible to grasp.

When he turned the corner, he saw Dave in his quarantine, alone in the guestroom on the back of the house. The blinds were down, but he could make out Dave's form, sitting in an armchair watching television, surrounded with a purple aura. Dave radiated purple. The color tinted the room. The noise had grown stronger as well. It was a line of sound, high and waving, sliding higher and lower but always returning to its home base. In some ways, it sounded like a machine. But he knew it was alive, and he kept searching for a better comparison.

Walking back to the car, he made the connection. It was like a whale song. He could still hear it almost a hundred meters from Dave's room, now that he was attuned to it. The sound of Covid, the Covid-song.

At home, he made ravioli. It was almost midnight, but he didn't think he could sleep. For their honeymoon, he and Mary traveled to Tuscany and took a cooking class in Florence. They learned how to make spinach-ricotta ravioli, tiramisu, and candied chestnuts. He didn't care for the chestnuts, but he paid careful attention to the way the chef made the ravioli, the way she kept spreading the dough with her roller, thinner and thinner. He noted the size of the squares, the way she pinched the edges together with the tines of her fork. Mary, on the other hand, showed little interest in the process, was almost continually a step behind, bugging him repeatedly for help.

"It's supposed to be fun," she said.

"I'm *having* fun," he said, though he was irritated, trying to learn the steps, making his own pasta and hers as well.

He didn't know what to do about this strange and special gift he had received. Possibly, he was the only person in the world who could see and hear the virus, but he had no idea what to do with this superhero-like ability. No one would believe him. He could wipe down surfaces, but that would make little difference. Scientists said it mostly spread through the air: a cough, a sneeze, droplets projected into the room and vacuumed into the next victim's lungs.

He dropped the raviolis into the pot. For a couple of minutes, he watched them swim. When he pulled them from the water, he had an idea.

As he ate, he began typing a letter. He stole a jpeg from a government website and used it for the letterhead. He had plenty of ink in his printer, and soon he was back in his car, circling town, cruising through neighborhoods, looking for the purple aura, listening for the frequency like a human radio. That night, he found four infected houses. He saw the aura before he heard it, until he reached the last house. That time he heard it first. He picked up the frequency and followed the sound, turning right at an intersection—and then, two houses from the corner, there it was. He dropped a letter in their mailbox marked with the seal of the state of Michigan, two bucks leaning against the coat of arms, and the Latin word, Tuebor, *I will defend.*

Driving home, he found the aura one more time at a twenty-four-hour pharmacy. When he drew closer, he saw that it was the pharmacist, a woman with long black hair, working the drive-thru, passing medicines to the sick.

The next morning, he called Mary and offered to run her errands. He promised to wipe down everything with sanitizer. He apologized for not being understanding the last time they talked. "This whole thing," he said, which had become a sort of catch-all explanation for why people were curt with one another, unproductive, or unresponsive. He didn't understand how Mary was managing to run errands with Agnes at home. He didn't really care if Mary left her alone for a little while. Germans gave their kids a lot more freedom and independence than Americans. But Mary, he knew, wouldn't feel comfortable.

"Thanks for the offer, but like I said, it's taken care of."

"How?" He was walking Otto, and his breathing was getting harder. He shifted the phone away from his mouth.

"Sometimes Zaza comes over and watches Agnes. We're the only people she ever sees." Zaza was Mary's mom,

Agnes's grandma. "That's our entire cohort," she added. "The three of us."

He had been awake for more than twenty-four hours when he finally went to bed, and, tired as he was, he thought about Zaza before he fell asleep. What he liked most about her was the way she always used the correct word for things. She was precise. She wouldn't say that a person "passed away;" she didn't rely on euphemisms. On the night of their wedding rehearsal, she spoke directly to Markus and Caroline. She said, "Welcome to the family." She used that word: *welcome*.

Markus slept on and off all day. When evening came, he drove to Detroit. Police cars sentineled interstate 94, stationed in the median every ten to twenty miles. Normally, as he approached Ann Arbor, the roadway filled, teeming with automobiles and tractor-trailers. Merging highways and never-ending construction meant slowdowns, at least, and often traffic jams. Today, he sailed through, listening to his music: Tom Waits, a perfect gravelly offering to the crumbling city. Behind the music, his tires transitioned from the new pavement to the old, from the hum of new asphalt to the rhythmic thud-thud of the old concrete, banging against every seam.

There were a handful of cases back in Coldwater, and so far, not a single death. After clearing all elective procedures from the docket, the nearest hospital in Battle Creek was quiet. A calm before the storm, a doctor said in the news. But Detroit was a disaster. Tens of thousands of known cases and tens of thousands more unknown due to a shortage of tests. Hospitals overflowing with patients, doctors working without proper P.P.E., under the overhanging fear that they would run out of ventilators, left to watch patients die without help.

Before leaving home, he printed out two hundred of his forged letters: "Authorities believe that a member of this household may have been in contact with an infected person or persons. Details at this time are not available. However, we ask you to take extra precautions and remain in self-isolation. Even if you are not experiencing symptoms, do not visit public spaces…"

He started in Dearborn near the high school and then jig-sawed through side streets, driving the speed limit, trying not to draw attention.

He expected to see the mess, but it wasn't like that; it was a matter of scale. The sick were still a small fraction of the four million people who lived in the Detroit area. At first, he found only a few auras here and there. Eventually, he found a cluster. He was driving through a neighborhood of century-old brick homes when he heard the Covid-song. On one street, four out of five houses glowed purple. The sound was a cacophony, four auras trying to shout over one another.

On the next street, a few more. Twenty in a radius of three or four blocks. He was just about to leave the area when a police siren erupted behind him.

"Scheisse," he said, pulling over.

He dug through his glove compartment and tried to think of a cover story. What if the police officer saw him opening mailboxes? Certainly, that was illegal.

It seemed to take forever before the police officer finally approached his open window. While he waited, his chest tightened.

"Out for a joy ride tonight?"

"Oh, no," he said.

"See I got a call about a sedan cruising the neighborhood, going real slow. Guessing that's you."

"I don't know about that."

The officer looked at him. "Where are you from?"

"Coldwater," he said.

"No, the accent," the officer said.

"I'm German," Markus said. "I've lived in the United States for eight years. I have a visa. I'm applying for a green card."

The officer was standing back from the open window, wearing a mask. He practically had to shout to be heard. "As a guest in this country. we expect you to follow our rules," he yelled. "I'm sure you wouldn't want a situation like this to impact your immigration status."

"My wife is asthmatic," Markus said. "I haven't been able to find a mask. I was looking all over."

"In the middle of the night?"

"I got tired and took a nap. I'm heading home now."

"Go home," the officer shouted. "We don't need wackos like you driving around our neighborhoods. We have enough problems already."

"Yes, sir. I totally understand, sir."

The officer gave him a written warning, and, still shaking, Markus drove away. It was three in the morning when he arrived in Coldwater. Exhausted as he was, he drove past Mary's. The road had recently been repaved, and he could hear the tread of his tires suctioning the street as he came to a stop. He stared at the dark house, sure that they were both sleeping. He felt as though he had been locked out of Agnes's life. He suspected that Mary was using the pandemic as an excuse to manage his interactions with his daughter. Given the opportunity, Mary would always take control.

He woke the next evening, a bright sun careening toward the horizon, the shadows bleeding together into an inky sea. He took some leftover ravioli from the fridge. The pieces were stuck together in a clump, and when he tried to pull them apart, they tore open, the cheesy guts falling out.

Otto was stir-crazy, and he tried to ignore his dog while

he checked his email. There was a message from Caroline, an evasive letter from the CEO of Kaffeeblitz about the company's future plans. He checked Facebook. So far Dave had been able to avoid the hospital.

Markus was utterly helpless. If the economy fell apart and he lost his job, he worried he would also lose his visa, which could mean leaving the country. It reminded him of the season when his marriage was ending. They tried counseling, but he knew Mary was done. It was like trying to stop a fall when there's nothing to hold onto.

It was evening, and he was fully awake, ready to start a day that had already disappeared. He peeked through his blinds and saw an empty street. Temperatures were dropping, and people were hunkering down for another night at home. He took out his guitar. When he was tired or stressed, Markus often reached for his guitar, picked and strummed, searching for chord progressions and licks he could use to build a new song. Sometimes, he hummed over the chords looking for a melody, and this time, something strange came out of him. It was the Covid-song.

It was unlike anything he'd ever written. It never would have occurred to him, under normal circumstances, to sing this way, offering these long brooding notes in falsetto, simple and straight-forward. Like a prayer.

Ever since he was a teenager in Bornheim, he had wanted

to move to the United States. All of the musicians he loved were American or had moved to the United States to play. The genre of music he loved most was called Americana. What was he supposed to do? Stay in Germany?

America didn't work out the way he expected. He landed in a small town in the Midwest, where he seemed to know more about American music than anyone he met. Fortunately, Ann Arbor and its folk scene wasn't too far away. He and Mary did take one trip to Nashville, where he saw two shows in the Ryman Auditorium. But now, in the throes of a pandemic, there were no concerts, no performances. He had been working on his own music for years, and he was struggling with his confidence. All he wanted was to make one really good album. Just one. He had yet to write anything that was really good. Some of his songs were sufficient, but it wasn't enough.

The next morning, he took Otto for a walk.

"Sorry, buddy," he said. "I'm doing the best I can."

It was cold again; grey clouds waded through the sky. The sun poked its head out for a moment but then tucked back into the cloud cover. He was just about to turn for home when he saw a dad and daughter playing in the grass. The dad was Markus's age, mid-thirties, and the girl was younger than Agnes, maybe four. They were racing, starting from an imaginary line, and running to the park bench, the dad pulling ahead and then slowing at the end, the girl running with straight legs, bouncing, laughing. She passed him every time, winning at the end. They both cheered, "Yay, yay."

The package was on the front porch when he got home. It was the size of a board game or a large puzzle. It was for Mary, sent to the wrong house. Immediately, he recognized the opportunity.

He drove to Mary's and knocked, stepped back from the door and waited. Nothing. Knocked again. No response.

How strange. Maybe Mary was in a meeting or indis-posed. Maybe she'd stopped answering the door. But he had a feeling, not unlike what he'd felt at Dave's house that night in the dark. He felt as if there was something he *needed* to find. He *needed* to keep looking.

Fortunately, he knew his way around the place. Their divorce had been difficult. Shoot, every divorce was difficult. But they never disintegrated. They tried to keep Agnes in mind and remain civil. When Mary was looking for a place to live, he went along and did the guy thing, made comments about some out-of-date wiring. He knew there was a door in the back of the garage that didn't close. It was warped from water damage, and the previous owner used a cinder block to keep it shut.

He rolled the block out of the way and opened the door. No car. Mary was gone.

He was hyperaware of his own presence as he entered the garage. He heard each footfall, his sneakers grinding against the dirty concrete. Light flooded into the room from the open door behind him, his shadow pitched in front of him, drawn in crisp lines, like a second person was moving with him toward the door to the house. He looked at the doorknob, confident it was unlocked, but unsure whether to continue.

That's when he heard Agnes. The sound was distant, but it was her. It sounded like she was crying. He grabbed the handle, turned the knob, eased the door open.

He had never seen this much Coronavirus. There was the infected gas station, but that was nothing compared to this. There was orange glow on the cabinet pulls, dishwasher, sink, faucet, countertop.

"Um Himmels willen." His heart raced.

He went to Agnes's room, avoiding the orange glowing blotches of living virus. As he approached, he realized that she was just talking to herself, probably playing with her dolls. Her guys, she called them. He didn't want to frighten her, so he spoke in as normal a voice as he could muster.

"Agnes, hi sweetie, it's Dad. I'm just here for a quick visit, mein Schatz. I haven't seen you in so long."

Her door also had the orange glow. On the doorknob, the edge of the door. He slid it open with his foot, and there she was. Her brown hair fell in curls to her shoulders.

"Hi sweetie." He got down on the floor, squatting on his knees.

She was holding a plastic horse in her hand, and she continued her conversation with the little animal.

"We never know'd that, did we?" she said. "We go'd all the way."

Finally, she looked at him.

"Dadda," she said. She lunged into him, wrapping her arms around his neck.

Markus didn't return her embrace. It was an instinct, built over the past month, of avoiding other humans. By the time he was ready to hug her back, reminding himself that she didn't have an aura, it was too late. She had picked up her toy horse and was explaining her made-up story.

"Mein Liebchen," he interrupted. "Where's Mama?" He put his hand on her shoulder, kissed the back of her neck. Her breath smelled like cereal.

"I'm playing with my toys," she said. Quite possibly, this was her explanation. She had been instructed to stay, to play with her toys. Mommy would be right back.

Moving quickly, he found bleach on a shelf in the laundry room. There was a clean rag under the sink, and he used it to turn on the water. He put in a stopper and ran the hot water, poured in the bleach.

Soon he was making progress. The kitchen took on the

thick smell of bleach, burrowing deep into his throat, and he imagined it was even cleaning the air, cleansing the whole house of virus. When he was done, he went to the living room. It wasn't as bad here. A few spots on the wall by the door, a light switch, a lamp.

Next the hallway. A closer inspection of Agnes's room, where he found a few more spots, one on the side of her bed, another on her dresser.

It was Mary. He was sure of it. She had brought the virus into the house. Soon, she'd come home, ringed in purple and unaware of her condition. She would undo his work, again spreading the virus all over the house. He couldn't bleach it out of her. He didn't even know how to tell her. *Mary, you need to get tested. Please just trust me.* He rehearsed the words in his mind.

When he heard the garage door surge to life, he went to the living room and sat down. He pictured her car rolling into the garage, Mary measuring space to the back wall. He waited.

As soon as she entered the kitchen, she started talking. "What's going on? What's that smell?"

"I'm in here," he called.

She entered the living room, moving cautiously, taking slow cat-steps. One, two, three. There was no aura.

"Markus, you scared the shit out of me."

She took another step forward. She shook her head. "I said no visits. This is totally inappropriate."

"Leaving our daughter unattended is inappropriate." He had her trapped. One time, a few months before the divorce, he got caught up in a conversation with a neighbor, and Mary found Agnes alone in the house. Even though he was there, right next door, Mary lost her shit.

Mary stopped moving. Her eyes were wide. She had big eyes, beautiful eyes. It was one of the things that attracted him. Those beautiful green eyes.

"Someone has the virus," he said.

She opened her mouth to speak but nothing came out.

"Is it Zaza?" he asked.

"I was just over there. I was trying to get her to eat."

"Why didn't you tell me?" He stood. He wanted to back away, but there was a wall behind him.

Agnes entered the room. Neither Mary nor Ages had an aura, but now, with both of them in the room, he could hear it. It was small. A thin line of sound. It made sense. It took time for the aura to appear, just as it took time for the glow to disappear. Agnes had the virus, and Mary had it, too. The virus was growing, reproducing inside its hosts.

"Do you know where she got it?" he asked.

Mary was crying. She shook her head. He wondered if it was the infected pharmacist.

"How is she?"

Mary fought back the tears. "She's running a fever. She's tired. I'm watching her oxygen levels."

"I don't know how to explain this," he said, "but I think I can help." Markus had theories. He believed that the aura grew deeper and stronger as the viral load increased. More virus also meant more sound. At the very least, he might be able to assess the severity of Zaza's illness. Also, he couldn't let go of the idea that he was given this ability for a reason. It had to be good for something.

Mary stared at him, and Agnes walked to her mother, grabbing her leg.

"You sell coffee makers," Mary said.

"Not anymore." There was nothing else to say, no way of explaining. "Good-bye, meine Lieben," he said, addressing them both.

His car was down the block. A brittle leaf scratched the street as it slid over the pavement. The wind was cold.

Zaza lived on the outskirts of town. It was a ranch style house on a county road, an acre parceled out from a farmer's field. There were a few small trees and a little landscaping, but it still looked like the house had been placed here by mistake. In early spring, the surrounding field was mud, dotted with last year's chaff.

Ever since he discovered the ability to see the virus, he had been trying to understand how it worked. He could see the virus glow; he could hear its song, if there was enough of it. He also seemed to be drawn toward the virus, as if by gravity. He felt it now, more strongly than he'd ever felt it before. The pull.

"Zaza," he called, as he let himself into the house. He was already heading for the bedroom, down a long hallway. Of course, there was Coronavirus everywhere, the bathroom door, the handle, blotches on the walls, though it was all faded, suggesting it had been a day or two since she was up, the virus gone stale like old bread.

This was his first time he was in such close proximity to a carrier, and he could see, not only the aura, but her breath. The virus inhabited the microscopic droplets that rose and fell with each squeeze of her lungs. It was like a little Covid-fountain, the world's strangest party trick.

"Zaza," he said. "Marilyn, it's Markus. I'm going to take care of you from now on."

He felt it again, drawing him toward Zaza. He crept forward while the Covid-song grew louder and clearer. There were layers of sound he'd never heard.

It had been years since he had been in this house, and he had only been in this room a couple of times. Somehow, though, it all seemed so familiar. The picture of Marilyn with her now-deceased husband on their wedding day. The walnut-colored bed frame. The matching dresser with its beveled mirror.

It was enough, seeing his reflection in the mirror, surrounded by infection like land mines, to wake him from his spell. Suddenly, he felt as if he couldn't breathe. He left the room, rushing down the hall and out the door. Outside, he was nearly gasping for air, as if he had been holding his breath underwater.

The sun was trapped behind a tide of clouds. He wrapped his arms around his chest, while the wind blew over the open fields, rushing into the side of the house.

There are things in life that are almost impossible to fully explain: why he proposed to Mary when there was that part of him that wasn't sure. Music. This was an impossible mystery—how it forged memories, could make people cry, and laugh, and dance. He couldn't understand why he was given this ability to see and hear the virus. Maybe he would never understand. But there was one thing he could do.

When he walked back into the house, he realized for the first time how warm it was, the heat turned up against Zaza's chills. She was asleep now, her breath light, her mouth closed. The only visible sign of her infection was the aura, deep purple against the white duvet.

He was no longer afraid. There was a chair on the other side of the bed. Mary must have put it there. He walked around the bed and sat down. He lifted the duvet and took her hand. Zaza looked older than he remembered.

At Zaza's bedside, he listened to the Covid-song. It was perfect. The melody soared, like a horn, playing without breath, leaving no space between notes. The last time he was in the room, he'd noticed the harmony, but it was more than a single note. It was a group of notes, perfectly balanced, like an orchestra made of pure sound. Without breath. Without strings and bows. Beneath the harmony was a base line, trembling and deep.

Markus began to sing. He didn't know how he knew the song, but he did. He knew where it was going, when it was lifting and retreating, when the chord changes were coming. The drive to sing was the same compulsion that kept urging him forward. He sang and sang, until the Covid-song reached its end.

Zaza woke, but she didn't speak.

He didn't have the wifi password, but there was enough cell service to stream music. From his phone, he played his favorite: Darlingside. Four voices woven together like thread into fabric.

Eventually, Zaza was able to sit. She was still weak, but she was able to talk a little. It seemed to Markus as if her aura was beginning to fade, though he wasn't positive. He walked around the room, looking from a different angle, making sure it wasn't just a trick of the light.

About the Author

Kevin Fitton is a writer, teacher, and musician. He has published a children's picture book, *Higher Ground*, with Caldecott-winning artist, Mary Azarian, along with a number of short stories in journals such as *Jabberwock, Limeston*e, and *The Saturday Evening Post.* He holds an MFA from the Writing Seminars at Bennington College and is pursuing a PhD from Western Michigan University.

Fomite

More story collections from Fomite...

Fomite

Ron Savage — What We Do For Love
Vince Sgambati — Undertow of Memory
Fred Skolnik— Americans and Other Stories
Lynn Sloan — This Far Is Not Far Enough
L.E. Smith — Views Cost Extra
Caitlin Hamilton Summie — To Lay To Rest Our Ghosts
Susan Thomas — Among Angelic Orders
Tom Walker — Signed Confessions
Silas Dent Zobal — The Inconvenience of the Wings

Writing a review on social media sites for readers will help the progress of independent publishing. To submit a review, go to the book page on any of the sites and follow the links for reviews. Books from independent presses rely on reader-to-reader communications.

For more information or to order any of our books, visit:

http://www.fomitepress.com/our-books.html

CPSIA information can be obtained
at www.ICGtesting.com
Printed in the USA
JSHW060408260822
29670JS00004B/21

9 781953 236685